ARCTIC STAR

TOM PALMER

Conkers

First published in 2021 in Great Britain by
Barrington Stoke Ltd
18 Walker Street, Edinburgh, EH3 7LP

www.barringtonstoke.co.uk

Text © 2021 Tom Palmer
Illustration © 2021 Tom Clohosy Cole

The moral right of Tom Palmer and Tom Clohosy Cole
to be identified as the author and illustrator of this work has
been asserted in accordance with the Copyright, Designs
and Patents Act, 1988

A CIP catalogue record for this book is available
from the British Library upon request

ISBN: 978-1-78112-971-5

Printed and bound by CPI Group (UK) Ltd, Croydon, CR0 4YY

Arctic Star is dedicated to Imperial War Museums and all its staff as a thank-you for all the help they have given to me and many other authors

The Arctic Convoy route from Scotland to Murmansk.

THE FIRST CONVOY

ONE

Norwegian Sea, October 1943

"You do know that some men who go out on deck to clear ice are never seen again, don't you?"

Frank took a deep breath, ignoring his friend Stephen's remark to focus on preparing himself for what was coming next.

The wind. The waves. The danger.

Frank had a hammer and chisel in one hand, while his other hand gripped the thick steel wire that ran the length of the ship from bow to stern. There for men to hold on to in rough weather. He could already feel its freezing cold metal through his

thick woollen Arctic gloves as the wind roared wildly around him.

HMS *Forgetmenot* rolled into another deep trough between waves, forcing Frank to reset his feet as the angle of the deck shifted again. And then his ice-chipping team were on the move. Frank, Joseph and Stephen staggered forwards into the storm, attached to each other by a rope – a lifeline.

Frank went first, ignoring the nausea of seasickness. He was immediately struck by a blast of wind so cold it was impossible to breathe. His lungs just couldn't take in the freezing air as he felt his feet slip underneath him on the icy deck. This was madness! But the lifeline did its job – as did his two friends. Frank stayed upright. Just.

Out in the open, the wild ocean rolled and roared and thumped at the side of the ship's metal hull. Frank felt grateful for the warm clothing of his

Arctic kit as shards of ice hit him like a hail of bullets.

There was a name for this ice, like there was a name for everything at sea. *Spindrift*. It was created as the wind whipped the surface water off the tops of the waves and froze it into hard sharp particles.

Frank flinched from the spindrift but kept moving. If he didn't, he knew that over the next hour ice would build up on the deck of the ship, freezing the guns, the lifeboats, the racks of explosive depth charges. Then HMS *Forgetmenot* would become top-heavy and capsize, pitching them all into the sea. The entire eighty-five-man crew would be dead in minutes.

Out of the corner of his eye, Frank could see some of the other forty-seven ships in their Arctic Convoy. No doubt junior sailors like him were having to do the same terrifying job on their decks as they all battled through the storm.

Frank kept his body low to help him balance as he approached the guard rail, which was like a metal fence that ran round the edge of the deck to prevent sailors from falling overboard. He glanced back to see Joseph holding on to his lifeline with a determined look on his face, then Frank began to attack the build-up of ice.

As he did so, the ship seemed to bounce off the waves, making it difficult to keep his footing and raise the hammer, then bring it down on the chisel. But Frank had to keep going. He'd found that work, keeping busy, was the best way to flush away his fear.

Further down the deck, he spotted three men operating a steam hose, melting the ice from around the mechanism of one of the ship's great guns. He figured a steam hose would be more effective than a hammer and chisel, but he would have to make do with what he had.

Using every muscle and sinew in his body, Frank focused on keeping his balance and driving his chisel into ridges of ice. He made good progress – chunks were coming away, some the size of his seaboots. He had the angle of the chisel right and was timing his strikes too, waiting for HMS *Forgetmenot* to crest a wave, then striking down with his hammer before the ship lunged into a trough. It was all about timing. That was the trick.

He took out another five or six large chunks of ice before it happened. One minute his hammer was raised to strike, the next the deck went from under him and he hit his back on something, his head on something else. Then he was falling, somersaulting downwards.

Instinctively Frank let go of his hammer and chisel, hoping they wouldn't spin into the air and take a lump out of him. Then he felt a sudden shock

of cold and wet. Took in a lungful of freezing salty seawater while trying to move his arms. But his heavy overcoat made that impossible and, really, Frank had no idea what was up and what was down, where the surface of the sea was, where the sky was.

But one thing he did now know: he was overboard.

In the sea.

Frank felt terror, his heart pounding inside his chest, his throat gasping for air. Submerged beneath the water Frank could feel his overcoat and boots becoming heavier and heavier, weighing him down, like there was a hand coming from the depths of the Norwegian Sea to drag him to his death.

As he fought for every breath, for his life, Frank could feel the cold the sailors had told him about when a man went overboard. A violent shivering. A numbness. The slowing of the heart.

It was a quick death, they had said. Not a terrible death, so long as you just gave in to it.

Soon Frank's exhaustion overcame him and he stopped fighting.

TWO

Plymouth, 1930s

During the years before they signed their papers
to join the Royal Navy, Frank, Joseph and Stephen
often found themselves on Plymouth Hoe, a piece of
high land that overlooked Plymouth Sound and the
Atlantic Ocean beyond.

The three sailors had been friends all their
lives. They had lived on the same street and attended
school together, on the edge of the Devonport Docks.
Despite his mum dying when he was just five, Joseph
had done well at school and passed his eleven-plus to
get into grammar school, unlike the other two.

But all three knew and loved the ships that they saw coming and going from the docks, the uniforms of the sailors, and had no doubts that one day they too would find themselves at sea.

Out of the three of them, Frank was the most devoted to the Royal Navy. He was one of the many Plymothians who had lost family at sea. But this didn't put him off signing up – if anything, it made him even more determined to serve.

Often, he would go alone to Plymouth Hoe when his two friends weren't able to play out. Without a dad at home and with a mum who had two jobs – one on the docks and another in a public house nearby – Frank had a lot of time to himself. Sitting at the foot of the statue of Sir Francis Drake, he would watch the ships of the Royal Navy coming and going through Plymouth Sound. He could identify any ship almost as soon as it appeared on the horizon.

HMS *Hood*. HMS *Norfolk*.

He knew them all. He even came to know the names of the ocean liners that took wealthy people on great adventures around the world. To America. To India. Australia, even.

When he was ten, Frank's mum had given him a sketchbook that his father had written and drawn in when he was a child growing up on the same streets.

The sketchbook had a hardback cover and was navy blue. Inside there were profiles of the great ships his dad had seen sail in and out of Plymouth.

As he grew older, Frank would sit on the same spot his dad was supposed to have sat on up on Plymouth Hoe, recording the names and shapes of today's fleet in the same way. Frank was careful to use the same type of pencil, style of shading and form of words as his dad. In this way he felt as if he was spending time with the father he had never met.

When Royal Navy vessels left Plymouth, Frank would often be joined on the Hoe by families. Young women and children, usually, waving wildly as the ships passed through Plymouth Sound, then faded into the distance, over the horizon, out to sea. When the ship was gone, the children would walk back into town with their mothers, shoulders slumped.

Frank knew their story. He had seen these events play out a hundred times. The woman's husband and children's father was going to sea to serve the King. They might not see him for months. They might not see him ever again. If they were unlucky.

And Frank had been unlucky.

His father had been a lookout on HMS *Firefly*, a gunboat that had been sunk on the River Euphrates in Iraq in 1924. He was killed before Frank's first birthday, just weeks before he was due to come home on leave to meet his son for the first time.

With only one parent each, Frank and Joseph became ever closer as they grew older.

Sometimes Frank sat near families who were waiting for their fathers to come home. He would hear them shriek and cry out when they saw what they thought was the right ship on the horizon and ask Frank to identify it. Was that the one they had been waiting for?

Frank was delighted when he could tell them: "Yes, that's your father's ship. He's coming home." Then he would show them the profile of the ship in his sketchbook and how it matched the one turning into the Sound.

Word got round. The boy with the sketchbook on Plymouth Hoe had the eyes to identify a ship the moment it became visible on the horizon. And it was true that his eyes were good. Very good. Just like his father's.

He liked the comparison.

One night he was watching ships arrive in the dark. It was summer 1940, just a week before the Luftwaffe came to bomb Plymouth so brutally for the first time. Frank spotted a large ship – a cruiser – ghosting in to Devonport. He wondered if it was HMS *Belfast*. He knew that the ship had recently hit a mine off Scotland and it was possible that it had come to Plymouth for a refit.

Frank didn't draw it in his sketchbook. Nor did he tell anyone he had seen it – not even his mother. The ship's arrival was clearly meant to be a secret and he knew to keep quiet.

Frank made fewer trips to the Hoe in 1941 as Plymouth was battered by the Germans. Wave after wave of bombers hitting schools, shops, churches, killing hundreds of people in their homes. Frank's mum wanted him home with her, so he

came to spend more time gazing at the framed
Royal Navy photographs of his father, grandfather,
great-grandfather and uncles. All in uniform. Part of
a family tradition of serving at sea.

So when his papers arrived through the
letterbox to confirm he had been accepted into the
Royal Navy, Frank had opened them and shown
them proudly to his mother.

"They're here," he said.

At first his mum snatched them off him and
held them over the fire. Then, pretending it was all a
joke, she handed them back to him and told him she
was proud, that his dad would have been proud too.

That moment – and the look of anger, then love,
on his mum's face – was Frank's last thought before
he lost consciousness and the freezing sea closed
over him.

THREE

Norwegian Sea, October 1943

"He's awake, sir."

Frank heard the muffled sound of a familiar voice as he emerged from the depths of unconsciousness. Felt a hand on his shoulder.

Joseph.

"And I think he's well, sir," Frank's friend added.

"He looks half-dead to me," a second voice joked. "But then he looked like that before he went in."

Stephen. Definitely Stephen. And Frank was pleased – his two friends were alive. And so, it seemed, was he.

"You're lucky this great oaf was on the other end of the lifeline," Stephen said, peering at Frank. "I'd have left you to the waves."

"Don't listen to him." Joseph shook his head. "He did just as much as me to get you out of the sea."

Frank smiled. Although he was confused, he understood that he was in the sickbay. And that he was safe onboard HMS *Forgetmenot*. It sounded as if Joseph and Stephen had saved him, hauling him out of the sea on his lifeline.

There were two bunks in the sickbay, tubes and wires hanging from the walls around them. The smell of disinfectant was sharp in his nostrils. Frank could see the ship's doctor with his back to them – heard him mixing something in a metal cup. He tried to sit up but felt Joseph's hand on his shoulder.

"Take it easy," Joseph said as the ship's doctor appeared at the bedside.

"How are you feeling, Ordinary Seaman?" the medic asked, handing Frank the cup.

Frank sat up cautiously. He still couldn't find a voice to reply.

"No need to rush," the doctor murmured. "You've had a shock. But thanks to this pair here, you're not at the bottom of the Norwegian Sea."

Frank turned to study his saviours.

"Thank you," he croaked as a fifth man entered the sickbay wearing a dark jacket with gold buttons and trim, and a blue and gold naval cap with a crown and anchor motif at its centre.

The captain.

Everyone stood to attention, except Frank, who fell back on his bunk.

"At ease, gentlemen. How's the patient?" asked the captain.

"He's fine, sir," Stephen said. "He decided not

to die alone overboard but to hold on for the next torpedo so we can all go together."

Captain Whitaker narrowed his eyes at Stephen. Stephen was already getting a reputation as a joker on board HMS *Forgetmenot*, but sometimes his bleak wartime humour was a bit too close to the bone.

The captain was an older man. Grey hair. A shadow of white stubble on his face. But his eyes were a sharp piercing blue, the colour of the sea when sunlight bounces off it.

"And how are our two heroes?" the captain asked, looking first at Joseph and then Stephen.

Frank's friends stood to attention again, chests puffed out.

"Good, sir. Thank you, sir."

"Well done, men. Credit to you both. The Master-at-Arms has filled me in and you'll receive extra rum tomorrow. With my thanks."

Frank watched his two friends salute Captain Whitaker, who now turned back to him and squatted next to Frank's bunk.

"Good morning, sir," Frank said.

"Good morning. How are you feeling, Ordinary Seaman?"

"Good, sir. Thank you."

"Well done. Take the next watches off. Rest. Recover. Understood?"

"Thank you, sir. But I'm fine, really. Please let me do my watches today. I don't need to rest."

Later, Frank returned to his mess – the deck where he and his friends slept in hammocks and ate at tables fastened to the metal floor with rivets.

All the way along the corridor and down the ladder from the sickbay, Stephen goaded him. "Please, sir, let me be on the watch ... sir ... sir ... please."

Frank ignored Stephen as he opened the door and was cheered into the mess.

Leading Seaman Bushell put his arm around Frank.

"We hear you were nearly fish food," he remarked, guiding Frank to his bunk. Frank's body ached all over from his struggle with the waves.

"Thanks to this pair, I'm not," Frank said, shuddering as he remembered how cold it had been in the water, how he had given up.

Frank accepted a leg up from the Leading Seaman and clambered into his hammock, then gave in to his exhaustion, letting the conversation below blend with the sounds of the sea pounding the sides of HMS *Forgetmenot*. He was asleep in seconds. He would need the rest so that he could be sharp for his next watch. They all would.

HMS *Forgetmenot* was about to enter the

dangerous waters of the Arctic Ocean, where German submarines and ships and aircraft lay waiting to attack the north-bound Arctic Convoys.

FOUR

Arctic Ocean, October 1943

By the end of Frank's afternoon watch the next day, darkness was already falling. The sun had travelled in a low arc against the pale sky and was slipping below the horizon. It was almost winter in the far north of Europe. The days were short. The nights were long.

Without the weak warmth of the sun, the temperature dropped rapidly. Freezing air burned Frank's face, turning his breath to vapour as he moved to the starboard side of the ship to get a good look at the convoy, the ships they were there

to protect. He was forced to squint as he put his binoculars to his eyes, the air was so cold.

Including the *Forgetmenot*, Frank counted six columns of eight ships, all of them tinted blood red by the setting sun. Twelve were Royal Navy. The other thirty-six, Merchant Navy, carrying 400 Hurricane aircraft, 500 tanks and countless tonnes of fuel and ammunition north towards Iceland, then east across the Arctic Ocean to the northern Russian port of Murmansk. Britain and its allies were arming the Russians so that they were able to fight back against the devastating Nazi invasion from the east.

Frank remembered a speech by Winston Churchill. He had said that the Russian danger was "our danger". Meaning that, because the Russians were enemies of Nazi Germany like Britain, they were now friends of Britain.

That logic was good enough for Frank. In fact,

most of what Churchill said was good enough for Frank. He'd hero-worshipped the Prime Minister ever since Churchill came to stand alongside the people of Plymouth in 1941 after it had endured weeks of bombing by the Germans.

Frank was startled from his thoughts by a voice behind him. A foreign voice. He spun round, his back to the sea.

If there was one thing that set him on alert it was a foreign voice. At home in Plymouth, living close to the Royal Navy base at Devonport, there was an anxiety about foreigners. They could be spies. Spies that could help the German air force – the Luftwaffe – decide where to drop bombs on his city.

But the voice behind him had not been that of a spy. It was Joseph, carrying two metal mugs of kye – a hot drink made by forcing a steam hose through huge blocks of chocolate in the galley.

"You made me jump," Frank said.

"Sorry." Joseph handed him a mug, which Frank accepted gratefully, the heat passing through his woollen gloves and into the palms of his hands.

"I was speaking in Russian," Joseph volunteered as the two young men leaned on the guard rail to stare out at the now grey sea and a sky drained of colour.

"Russian? How do you know Russian?" Frank asked.

"School. We had a teacher at the grammar school – Dr Page. He was a big fan of Russian. He offered it as an extra course. But I did a lot of it at home, myself."

"I had no idea," Frank said, surprised there was something he didn't know about his friend. "I knew you spoke French and German. So what did you say just then? In Russian?"

"I was pointing out the North Star. It's the one dead ahead. Russian sailors use it to navigate the Arctic. Some of them actually call it the Arctic Star."

Frank nodded and stared at the star. Its light seemed to be pulsing as he reflected briefly on his friendship with Joseph.

When Joseph had gone to the grammar school, Frank had thought he would make new friends there – posh and clever friends – and would forget about Frank. So he'd been pleased when instead they'd stayed in touch and continued to see each other out of school.

But although they'd remained close, Frank had always felt a bit resentful about the grammar school. There was something intimidating about his friend going to the best school in Plymouth.

Frank looked at Joseph again. "Why did you choose Russian, though? What's the point?"

"I like Russia," Joseph explained. "It's interesting. They do things differently."

"Like what? I don't understand."

"There are no rich and poor in Russia," Joseph explained. "Everyone is equal and they share everything. They have no royal family. And their leader, Joseph Stalin, makes sure they stay equal."

Frank had heard that the Russian royal family had been murdered and all their money and jewels taken by soldiers. It didn't sound like something to be glad about.

"In fact," Joseph volunteered, "I think I'd rather be Russian than English."

Frank stared at Joseph. He couldn't imagine what it would be like not to want to be English and he couldn't stop himself challenging his friend.

"I think I'll stick with Churchill and the King," he said.

"Churchill?" Joseph scoffed. "You've always loved him. But that's because you don't know the truth about him."

Frank felt a flush of heat to his head and raised his voice to ask, "What's that supposed to mean?"

"Churchill is an idiot," Joseph said. "He's a warmonger and every battle and war he has been involved in has ended in disaster."

As he listened to Joseph, Frank leaned against the guard rail and felt his stomach heave. They had been at sea for four days and he was still feeling seasick, like sailors often did for the first week of a voyage.

He put his hand to his throat. The nausea was worse again now the seas were building. But Frank still wasn't prepared to let Joseph away with this.

"You can't speak about Mr Churchill like that," he said.

"I can," Joseph said, defiant. "We've had this argument before, Frank."

Frank noticed that Joseph looked a bit green now, his skin damp. The sea was getting to him too.

"He's a war hero," Frank went on, still feeling outraged no matter how many times they had discussed it. "He's our leader."

Joseph staggered towards the guard rail just as Frank saw Stephen arrive with his own mug of kye.

For a few seconds none of them spoke as Joseph choked and coughed, then held both hands to his face, something dark coming from his mouth as he leaned over the rail, a torrent of brown kye-stinking sick spewing over the side.

And suddenly the stench of bile and chocolate was too much, forcing Frank to stumble to the guard rail, beside Joseph, then lean over to vomit into the sea.

He turned when he heard what he thought was laughter and looked over to see Joseph's eyes smiling. Stephen came to steady them both, gripping their arms in case they fainted and toppled overboard.

Then, inexplicably, the three of them were laughing. Laughing hard as their small ship – with eighty-two other sailors on board – rode the waves towards Russia, to within easy range of the Luftwaffe and to seas where the U-boat wolfpacks hunted night and day, waiting for the chance to kill British sailors, regardless of whether they loved Winston Churchill or not.

FIVE

For the rest of the time before the morning watch, the three friends took shelter below deck in their mess. While some of the other men slept in hammocks strung from large metal hooks welded into the ceiling, Frank and Joseph sat at one of the tables playing Uckers, a board game the sailors enjoyed. Stephen was next to them, watching. He put his hand against the inside of the hull of the ship and smiled.

"Do you know how thick this is?" he asked Frank.

"What?" Frank muttered.

"This sheet of metal between us and billions of tonnes of freezing water."

"How thick?" Frank asked, still focusing on the Uckers board. He knew Stephen's question was the set-up for a joke.

"One inch," Stephen said. "That's it. One inch between us and oblivion."

Frank glanced at Stephen. His friend was bored. He had a restless look about him.

"I mean … if you think about it, there must be … maybe ten ways we could be killed right now." Stephen was grinning, on the verge of laughter. "Do you think we could do it? Think up ten ways to die?"

Nobody replied.

"A U-boat torpedo through here," Stephen said, starting to answer his own question. "That's one. It would penetrate the hull here, then explode once it knocked your game off the table. I mean … we'd see

it for a split second before the water came gushing in and we were all blown into a million pieces."

"Shut it," said a sleepy voice from one of the hammocks above.

But Stephen didn't shut it. He had more to say.

"A torpedo, but this time from a German seaplane dropping out of the clouds. Or a Stuka, screaming down and dropping a pair of bombs on the bridge. A mine laid by the Nazis. A storm so wild the ship just doesn't come back up from under a giant wave. We just disappear, like we never existed.

"Ice on the deck becoming so heavy that it capsizes us. A collision with another ship in the convoy. And then – a special one for us in the engine room – if there's a fire, the captain opening the drenching gear and drowning me and the other engineers. That's what happens, you know. The engine room is filled with seawater to give you lot a chance to jump onto a life

raft and get away before the ship explodes. We get locked in the engine room as it fills up with water. That's the best one yet. How many are we up to now?"

"Eight," Frank said. He shuddered, glad he wouldn't ever have to face the result of Captain Whitaker's decision to open the drenching gear.

"Eight ways to die," Stephen said. "Come on, let's get it up to ten. This is much more fun than Uckers."

Frank heard soft laughter from above. He looked up and saw Leading Seaman Bushell looking down as they heard the thunderous banging of the sea against the side of the ship.

"The *Scharnhorst*," the Leading Seaman suggested. "The German battleship. One of its eleven-inch shells could split us in two. We're bound to meet it one day. If the U-boats don't get us first."

"Brilliant," Stephen said. "An eleven-inch shell. Just brilliant. One more and we're all winners."

Frank felt himself laughing now. "Iceberg strike," he said.

And Stephen was on his feet, jumping and cheering.

"We did it!" he cried. "Ten ways to die. We win."

The Uckers game resumed in silence once the laughter had stopped.

What was it about Stephen? wondered Frank. He could bring you out of yourself, cheer you up, but when you'd stopped laughing, you felt even worse than you did before.

He began to prepare for his watch. It wouldn't be long before they were all back on duty – Frank and Joseph on lookout, Stephen down below in the belly of the ship, feeding the engines, trying not to think about the captain opening the drenching gear.

Frank shivered. He'd put his layers on now. It would be cold up there on deck. With every watch

they were further north. Colder and darker as they moved into the Arctic waters.

Stephen grinned as he observed Frank putting all his clothes on. He was wearing a boiler suit. One layer.

"I feel so sorry for you lads up on deck," he laughed. "All the ice. All that sea. Down in the engine room it's like high summer every watch."

Frank shivered again. He knew that when he was up there, on the deck, exposed to the waves, the spindrift, the wind and icy air, he would think of how warm Stephen was and feel intense envy. But he had to face it. Do his duty. Like his dad, his uncles and his grandad before him.

SIX

The officer on his deck nodded as Frank took up his position. There was a layer of high cloud as they sailed east on the Arctic Ocean above the top of Scandinavia. The wild anger of the wind and waves was no more. Frank felt as if the sea was resting, like some enraged creature that had worked itself up, then calmed, maybe sleeping before its next outburst.

But it was cold. Freezing cold.

Frank liked his lookout post on the starboard side. His was the surface watch, which meant looking out across ninety degrees of sea from the lowest

deck, using his binoculars to scan the dark waves, searching for the periscope of a U-boat, the shape of a mine bulging under the swell, or even a torpedo skimming towards the hull of the ship. Some of the ten ways to die that Stephen had described earlier. Other men would be watching the skies for Condors and Stukas, the enemy's aircraft.

Frank felt stiff and uncomfortable in his Arctic kit, but he knew he had to wear everything he could on lookout now. That meant woollen long johns, a polo-neck jersey, trousers, overalls, an itchy woollen duffel coat, thick mittens, stockings, heavy seaboots, gloves and a scarf. These layers of clothes were meant to keep the sailors warm. And if you stayed dry, they worked.

On a previous watch he'd heard a noise that one of the older sailors had said was a whale. A bit like a bird calling, but deeper, more resonant. He only

heard it that once, on a quiet night, in the dark. But it had stayed with him. So, as he scanned the sea, he watched for whales too. He would like to hear one again.

Frank tried not to be distracted by flashing lights as the ships in the convoy communicated. They spoke to each other night and day, not via radio but in Morse Code using lights called Aldis lamps. Radio could be picked up by German U-boats or spotter planes and that would bring danger.

The ocean was vast. For an enemy submarine to find the convoy – even one this large – was like searching for a lost coin among a thousand pebbles on a beach. But if you used the radio – and they heard you – they could find you. And sink you.

An hour into his watch, a faint droning drifted in and out of Frank's consciousness above the sound of

the sea and the ship's engines. He wiped the lenses of his binoculars as the sea spray was beginning to obscure his vision. What was that?

When he heard the noise a second time, he turned his binoculars upwards. There was nothing there apart from the high cloud with the occasional gap where he could see the Arctic sky, so he went back to his surface watch. Those on the bridge would be on the lookout for aircraft. That was not his duty.

But then the droning noise came a third time. Louder now. It was an engine. Definitely an engine.

Frank put his binoculars down and scanned the sky using his naked eyes. The faint buzzing was intermittent, but he kept looking up, blocking out all other sounds.

And then he saw it.

A fleeting vision of a shape in a blue patch between clouds. Silver glinting, catching the sun.

Then a silhouette. He'd seen it for half a second at most. But he'd seen it. He was sure. Four engines. Thick wings tapering. Blunt nose.

A Condor.

Frank knew very well that the Condor was a reconnaissance aircraft the Germans used to search for enemy ships.

"Focke-Wulf Condor spotter plane to the starboard side. Above the cloud cover," he reported to the officer still standing in position along the deck.

"Are you certain?" the voice came back.

Frank gazed up at the gaps in the clouds. The sound had faded. He had seen the Condor only once. But he was sure. He trusted his eyes more than anything. And he'd heard it too.

"Certain, sir. Yes, sir."

The officer spoke into the tube, a communication device behind him. Two seconds later the alarm bell

rang: Action Stations on board HMS *Forgetmenot*. The ship's horn sounded too, passing the news on to others in the convoy as Frank kept his eyes on the skies. The sight and sound of the Condor had gone now and he was starting to doubt himself. Had he caused men on dozens of ships to go to Action Stations for nothing? Had he endangered the convoy, making it sound its horns and reveal its whereabouts to German U-boats?

Nothing for a minute.

And then – through a break in the clouds – the Condor could be seen by everyone. Frank felt relieved – he'd not made a mistake. But his relief was followed by shock as the noise of hundreds of anti-aircraft guns deafened him. It was the first time the convoy had opened fire since leaving home.

Covering his ears, Frank could see the tracer fire of bullets shooting up towards the Nazi spotter

plane that was now arcing away to return to the mainland.

It had done what it was there to do.

It had spotted the convoy.

As it turned, the co-pilot would be radioing back to base to summon an attack. But what kind of attack?

No one knew. Frank ran through some of the scenarios that Stephen had mentioned.

Dive bombers.

Torpedo aircraft.

U-boats.

They could all be on their way. It might take a few hours, but it was only a matter of time. They would come.

The officer who had passed on Frank's spot to the bridge put his hand on Frank's arm.

"They want you on the bridge," he said. "Next watch."

"Yes, sir."

An attack was incoming. And the captain needed him. Frank felt a mixture of pride and fear. Pride that he was useful. Fear about what might happen next.

SEVEN

When the next watch began, Frank took up his position on the starboard side of the bridge, wiped his binocular lenses dry and began to scan the sea. It was a different sea to his last watch: wild, with freezing water thrashing the decks. Frank shivered.

Being up on the bridge felt like he was on another ship altogether. This was where all the decisions were made. The bridge was on the top deck and towards the front of the ship, so that the captain, his officers and a team of lookouts had the best view of the sea and the sky. And now Frank was part of that team.

But this was no time for pride. Frank knew he had to feel fear. Controlled fear that would help him to focus as he scanned the waves for periscopes and the hint of a U-boat silhouette. He had a job to do. And he had to do it well.

Up high he could see the whole convoy as it staggered through the storm, great surges of white spray exploding from the sides of tankers and freighters as they were pounded by the waves. When HMS *Forgetmenot* dipped into a trough, it appeared as if there was a wall of water towering over them, before the ship began to climb the next peak, lunging from side to side as it moved to the contours of the ocean.

Being so much higher above the waves, the bridge moved with a more exaggerated – and sickening – motion, the deck sloping to one side, then to the other. At one point Frank vomited over

the side. But nobody said a word. These things were normal.

HMS *Forgetmenot* – a flower-class corvette – was there to protect the convoy, its size and shape allowing it to weave among the ships and identify the deadly threat of U-boats before they unleashed torpedoes. This gave Frank the chance to see the decks of some of the freighters, where he spotted tanks lined up like children's toys on a table.

But as darkness fell, it was harder to see the other ships. They were ordered to black out in the same way families were in their homes back in Plymouth, but visibility was most affected by the storm. With the sea and wind in turmoil, it was like the air was half water.

Drenched to the skin, Frank had never imagined seas like this. He was no longer *watching* the waves and the sea – he was *among* them, part

of them as they crashed and collided, shouldered into the ship, loomed over them like a range of mountains about to collapse.

The ship would pitch into a trough, bows down, as if they were about to dive beneath the sea, then it would correct itself, screw to the side and rise on the next wave, a great onrush of water flooding the decks, then pouring back into the ocean. The noise was deafening as hundreds of tonnes of ship were hit by thousands of tonnes of water.

Frank wanted to cover his ears, but he had to hold on to the guard rail that ran around the bridge for fear of losing his balance and being swept away by the water cascading over him. There was no cover on the bridge – it was open to the air. No roof. No ceiling. No windows. Just the sea and the sky and a handful of men.

Frank tried to watch the seas for U-boats, but it

was next to impossible as the salt stung his eyes and his binoculars banged against his face.

But still HMS *Forgetmenot* moved at speed among the lumbering cargo ships of the convoy. Frank saw how – weighed down with freight – some of the larger tankers barely moved in the heavy seas. They just forged on, slow and steady, somehow managing to avoid colliding with each other in the storm.

Even though he kept his eyes on the surface of the sea, Frank occasionally spotted the Arctic Star Joseph had told him about as clouds scudded across the canvas of the sky. His mind drifted, imagining Russian sailors navigating these treacherous waters in ships made from trees and animal skins in times before maps and signal lights. The star must have meant everything to them – it was beginning to mean something to him.

Frank scanned the sea, left to right, right to left, keeping his eyes on the black inky water. He saw nothing. It was so dark. Pitch-black.

Then he spotted a flash of white. A trail in the water. Not a wave. Not a whale.

"A torpedo," Frank called out, then heard loud voices behind him, the captain shouting orders to the engine room. He felt the ship lunge to the side in an attempt to avoid the incoming missile.

The officers on the bridge joined Frank on the starboard side to watch the torpedo skim past the hull of the HMS *Forgetmenot*, missing them by just a few metres. Now the Action Stations bells were ringing on board and the ship's horn was booming the message across the miles of sea the convoy was covering, Aldis lamps relaying messages, spreading the panic.

Frank was shocked by the sound of dozens of

running feet in the corridors and on stairways – a stampede as the men of HMS *Forgetmenot* knew they had two minutes to go from eating or sleeping to be ready for war.

The captain was screaming on the radio at the tanker to their port side. An oil tanker. Slow and huge. The next object in the path of this torpedo.

It had no chance. Frank could see that.

The captain called out, "Shield your eyes."

Then a ball of fire and light, a noise like thunder. But louder. A thousand times louder. A burst of warm air like a sudden wind, hot and stinking of metal and oil.

Frank turned his back to avoid looking at the blast, to keep his eyes good for the dark, as the captain had asked. All he could see was a projection of what was going on behind him on the surface of the sea and on the clouds. A massive ship carrying a

million gallons of oil exploding. Land at least thirty miles away was illuminated.

HMS *Forgetmenot* manoeuvred to the spot where the captain calculated the U-boat that released the torpedo might have dived. And now came the rattle of depth charges being released. Everyone on board knew what was coming next: these explosives would drop to a certain depth, then the water pressure would set them off. The ship vibrated beneath their feet as the depth charges detonated.

Frank kept scanning the seas, on the lookout for more danger, not able to give a moment's thought to the stricken tanker and its small crew who would now be drowning, burning or freezing to death. He couldn't afford to think about them now. He needed to worry about his own ship.

EIGHT

Barents Sea, October 1943

The sea was calm now that they were approaching the vast Kola Inlet, the wide estuary that led thirty miles inland to Murmansk. There were massive air-defence guns on either shore to fend off aerial and submarine attacks on the Russians' Arctic port.

Frank stood on deck watching dozens of shapes low in the water ahead. Ships from other convoys waiting to leave for the journey south.

A week after the U-boat attack, HMS *Forgetmenot* and the rest of the convoy had made it safely to Russia without any more casualties, but Frank would never

forget what he had witnessed, or escape the knowledge that none of those on board the tanker had survived.

He stared out at the land in front of them. At Russia. This was the country they were here to help, supplying it with tanks and planes and fuel. He felt proud that Britain was able to assist a nation so much larger than itself.

Above the land, clouds seemed to be moving strangely. Wrapped up again in all his kit, a scarf tight around his face to keep out the extraordinary cold, Frank stared upwards. Why were the clouds swirling, even glowing?

"We're not far from Murmansk," Joseph said, appearing on deck with Stephen, the three friends staring at the first foreign country they had ever seen.

"And the Communist paradise of Russia, also known as the USSR," Stephen added.

"That's right." Joseph grinned.

Frank wondered if Joseph realised that Stephen was mocking him.

"I am so excited," Joseph carried on. "We'll have shore leave. Can you imagine? I can speak to the Russians in their own language. We can see their buildings, their streets, how they live. Aren't you excited?"

Frank smiled. His friend's enthusiasm was infectious.

"Some of the lads in the engine room have been to Russia before," Stephen warned. "Be prepared to come away disillusioned, Uncle Joe."

Frank heard Joseph breathe in sharply, then saw him shake his head.

"You don't know what you're talking about. It's not just a country, Stephen," Joseph snapped. "It's … it's a way of life. A new way of life. You'll see. When we get there."

Frank nodded. He was half interested and half worried by what Joseph was saying. Could another country really be so different? Would everyone be walking around with smiles on their faces? No rich? No poor? Did they really share everything? It did sound good.

"*You'll* see," Stephen told him. "But I won't spoil it for you. You can judge for yourself."

"I will."

"Good."

Joseph turned away from Stephen to Frank. "Let me teach you some Russian?"

"Yes," Frank agreed. "Teach me to say *Hello, how are you?* I can be friendly at least."

Now the three friends were laughing again as Frank and Stephen struggled with the challenges of the Russian language, the sound rippling across the waves towards the land. Either side of the ship

they could see the silhouettes of hills in the eerie half-light.

And as HMS *Forgetmenot* sailed south into the Kola Inlet, Frank saw the strange clouds evolve from grey to swirling greens and purples.

Stunned, he jabbed at Joseph.

Joseph looked at him, then at the colour in the sky around them. His face was beaming.

"The aurora borealis," Joseph gasped.

"What?" Frank asked.

"Also known as the Northern Lights," Joseph explained. "They're made by particles from the sun mixing with gases in the earth's atmosphere and lighting up the sky. People used to think it was the light from campfires or torches of the gods before science explained it."

The three young men gazed up in awe as they watched the sky gyrate with greens and purples, like

58

a dozen rainbows twisting and turning in the Arctic night, while the HMS *Forgetmenot* sailed on towards Murmansk on the calmest seas of the journey.

As HMS *Forgetmenot* eased down the Kola River into Murmansk, a light snow settled on the deck. From a distance, the Russian city looked to Frank like a scene from a Christmas card. Painted wooden houses with snow-topped mountains behind them. Perfect columns of smoke rising in a breezeless sky.

Apart from the faintly musical clanging of a crane unloading a ship, Russia's most northerly city was quiet, silhouetted figures visible walking against the snowy backdrop. It *did* look idyllic and Frank wondered if Joseph was right about Russia.

Within seconds of the ship docking, a small group of Russian men wearing long coats and furry hats swiftly boarded HMS *Forgetmenot*, very serious

expressions on their faces. Frank was not surprised by this. What was more important than bringing war materiel to one of Britain's main allies? What was more important than defeating Nazi Germany? This wasn't a game.

"Right, shore leave," the Master-at-Arms said to Frank, Joseph and Stephen a few minutes later. "You are up first. You have four hours. Then back on your watch. Understood?"

The Master-at-Arms was a big man with broad shoulders and huge hands. He was responsible for discipline on the ship, acting as the ship's policeman.

"Yes, sir," Frank replied.

"And please be aware that there are strict rules here," the Master-at-Arms went on, glancing at the group of Russian officials who were still talking to the captain. "*Don't* fraternise with the locals. *Stay* in groups or pairs. This is another country; they do

things differently here. That welcoming committee up there will have been quite clear: you break any of their laws, you're down in the salt mines for five years. Understood?"

Joseph let out a short laugh.

The Master-at-Arms studied him, then glanced at Stephen. "Tell him, will you? I assume the lads in the engine room have told you about our last trip here?"

Stephen put his hand on Joseph's shoulder. "Please don't concern yourself, sir. Comrade Joseph would be proud to serve in the salt mines. But I'll do my best to keep him from that heroic fate."

Everyone laughed. But Frank was forcing it. He was worried. He didn't like the idea of salt mines. He was about to visit a foreign country for the first time in his life and he was nervous.

The Master-at-Arms' warning had alarmed him.

They do things differently here.

SHORE LEAVE

NINE

Murmansk, Russia, October 1943

Despite his worries, Frank was delighted to be off the HMS *Forgetmenot*. His first voyage – first convoy – at sea had unsettled him and he craved dry land. He didn't want to admit it to himself, but, after what they had been through, a part of him was afraid of the sea now.

As they walked down the gangway – wrapped up in duffel coats, scarves and hats to keep out the cold – Joseph grinned. He held his two friends back just before they were about to step off the ship and onto the dock. Frank and Stephen let him have his moment.

"Mother Russia," Joseph beamed, then placed his foot on the dock. "You know that Murmansk means 'the edge of the world' in Saami, the local language?"

Frank was astonished by all the things Joseph knew.

As they walked along the harbourside, Joseph called out "*Dobroe utro!*" – Good morning! – to any of the dockers he saw. But none of them seemed to hear him.

Frank was surprised to see the dockers dressed in very basic clothes. Rough jackets and trousers. No overcoats like the one he had on. And even wearing that, he was feeling the cold. The locals must be freezing. But maybe they were used to it?

As they reached the gates and sentry boxes they needed to pass through to leave the docks, they were asked to show their papers to a tall Russian guard: a woman, wearing a fur hat with a red star

over her forehead, who pointed her gun at them as they approached.

Stephen put his hands up and grinned.

"*Spasiba*." Joseph thanked the woman as she handed their papers back, still studying them through narrowed eyes.

Frank sensed mistrust from the woman. Perhaps she wanted to know why this English sailor was speaking Russian. He wondered if that was a problem – if it made them stand out. But Joseph missed it, like he seemed to miss the poor state of the dock workers' clothing.

"Look at this place," Joseph enthused. "The guards and, over there, the workers. Half of them are women. Do you see what I meant? The Russians, they don't see men and women as different. Rich. Poor. Male. Female. Everyone is equal. Everyone is a worker."

Frank nodded, looking around at the foreign

scene. He felt confused, seeing Murmansk through his own eyes but also through Joseph's. It was true that you didn't see women working on the docks in Plymouth. But did that make things better here?

They walked on. Into the city. Past clusters of wooden buildings that looked like houses. Two- and three-storey concrete buildings which could have been offices. And large wooden warehouses, almost like the ones you saw in Plymouth. Military vehicles, closed trucks, edged along the rough earthen roads.

On the sides of two low wooden buildings they saw posters of a large-faced man, black hair slicked back, a fierce look in his eyes, but with a smile on his lips.

"Joseph Stalin," Joseph told Frank, gleeful. "They all have pictures of him in their homes, too."

"His gloriousness, Comrade of comrades, Uncle Joe," Stephen added.

Frank noticed that Joseph ignored the jibe.

At the side of the road groups of people sat round small open fires, dropping what looked like grass into boiling water. One man was cutting a large loaf of black-coloured bread. He was using a saw, Frank noticed, trying not to stare.

And as they went, Joseph continued to greet people in Russian, but still very few responded. Some stopped to stare. One man even spat on the ground.

But Joseph took it in his stride, reacting like a tourist having a day out in London.

"You just don't see it, do you?" Stephen raised an eyebrow. "This place is a catastrophe, Joseph. It's a hell hole. They eat grass soup. The people working on the docks are as good as slaves. This town – look – it's bombed out and messed up. And you need to stop greeting people in your grammar-school Russian.

You probably sound like their last Tsar. And you know what happened to him."

"Oh, typical," Joseph interrupted. "The Englishman abroad. With only negative things to say about another country."

"We'll see," Stephen muttered.

They walked on. Some of the pavements seemed to be made of loose wooden boards. After tripping over one, Frank looked behind them and, as he recovered himself, he saw three men. Possibly following them.

He remembered what the Master-at-Arms had said about the salt mines and being careful. Had he been serious after all? Were they in danger?

TEN

Worried now, Frank began to walk faster past the low wooden buildings, along roads piled with crumbled pieces of concrete, hoping Joseph and Stephen would take the hint and speed up.

Growing up in Plymouth – another naval town – they knew you had to keep your wits about you in places like this.

"What's the rush?" Joseph complained.

"We're being followed," Frank told him.

Stephen looked back, then frowned. "He's right ... Come on, Comrade." He urged Joseph on. "We've got the secret police in tow."

But Joseph was smiling contentedly, not sensing danger as he gazed around at the buildings and people. He continued to greet anyone they passed in Russian. He was drawing attention.

"He's in a fantasy world," Stephen joked to Frank.

"Joseph?" Frank tried to get his friend's attention.

"What?" Joseph asked, irritated.

"I'm not sure the locals like you talking Russian to them. It's making them suspicious. And those men are still following us. Do you think we should keep to ourselves a bit more?"

Joseph let out a laugh. "I didn't come all this way through all those storms and Germans to keep to myself. This is my dream—"

"I know, but can you tone it down? We need to be careful."

Frank watched his friend frown and immediately felt bad that he was taking some of the pleasure away from Joseph's big day out in Russia.

The three sailors made their way into a square with low buildings on all sides, some of them burned out, with charred wood and shattered windows, glass on the floor. A woman standing at a brazier in the centre of the square was roasting something and selling it in wraps of paper.

Without hesitating, Joseph walked up to her confidently, keen to try out his Russian again.

"Joe," Frank called after him, surprised to hear a touch of anger in his own voice. But Joseph ignored him.

At first the woman seemed excited to meet them, offering to sell them each a wrap of whatever it was that she was roasting.

But as the exchange with Joseph went on, Frank

noticed that the woman's manner started to change. She began to look around her, as if she was worried she was being watched. When she saw the three men who had been walking behind Frank, Joseph and Stephen, she took the handlebars of her trolley and began to wheel it away from the sailors, looking back warily.

Stephen laughed. "You need to work on your chat-up techniques, Uncle Joe. What were you telling her?"

Joseph looked embarrassed. And angry.

Frank understood that his friend's feelings were hurt. This was not the hero's welcome Joseph had hoped for. The fact that an Englishman could speak Russian meant nothing to these people. That was clear. It was clearer still that his behaviour was attracting attention, creating suspicion. Frank recalled what the Master-at-Arms had said. This was

a different country. They did things differently here. And he began to boil with anger at his friend. They could be in real danger if Joseph carried on like this.

And then, very suddenly, the friends found themselves surrounded by the three men Frank had spotted when he tripped earlier. The ones he had thought were following them. The ones Stephen had said were secret police.

The first man was talking rapidly at Joseph, jabbing his finger at his chest.

These people, whoever they were, seemed to know that Joseph could speak Russian. And they didn't like it.

Joseph looked rattled as he listened.

"Papers," he gasped at last. "We need to show them our papers."

"We just did. At the docks," Frank said.

"Frank. Just do it," Joseph snapped.

The three young sailors stared at the pistol the Russian was now holding down by his leg and quickly handed their papers over. The man gave the papers a brief glance, shook his head, then pocketed them inside his coat and said something in hard angry Russian to Joseph.

Joseph's face drained of colour. He turned to Frank. Frank could see his friend had been stripped of all his clever thoughts. He looked like a frightened little boy now.

"He says ... he says we have to go with him."

"What?" Frank felt a rush of panic flush through his body as one of the men grabbed his arm, tearing at his shoulder. He saw Joseph's arms being taken too. And Stephen's.

"This way," the Russian said in English, pulling Frank in the direction of a dark alley between two buildings.

Frank looked wildly at his friends. He couldn't catch his breath to speak, his arm hurt so much from being wrenched out of its socket.

ELEVEN

The three young men found themselves being dragged at gunpoint down a dark alley.

Arms twisted behind their backs, they were immobilised by pain. And the echoes of their footsteps felt ominous as they were forced into a second enclosed square, a courtyard with black iron gates that screeched open, then clanged shut behind them.

They were trapped.

The man holding Joseph frowned, then flung him to the floor, spitting on him. Now he lit a cigarette and exhaled the smoke high into the

darkening Russian sky. He laughed, said something to his comrades, then kicked Joseph hard in the ribs, slipping on the icy floor as he did so, falling, his gun skittering across the ice.

Frank and Stephen took their chance and unleashed a storm of punches and kicks, Stephen knocking one of their captors senseless with his first punch. And with Joseph back on his feet, it was now three against two, which made all the difference.

For Frank, it brought back memories of fights with children from other schools back home in Plymouth. Scrapping as a team to get out of trouble if they ended up in the wrong part of the city.

They kicked and punched until there was no more resistance from the three men on the floor, their hands over their heads, their legs curled up. The gun their leader had been waving was still lying a few metres away, out of their reach.

It was over. Frank picked up the gun and pocketed it as the trio stopped to look at what they'd done.

"We need to get out of here," Joseph said.

The other two nodded.

Then Frank remembered something. "Our papers!" he said, stooping to reach inside the pocket of the man who'd taken them. The man grunted as he began to come round.

"Genius." Stephen smiled.

Then they were running. Opening the squealing gate. Through the alley, a storm of footsteps. Feet hard on the uneven streets. Stephen taking the lead, calling back, "Come on! Faster!"

They didn't want to give the men time to recover, to follow them, to sound the alarm. They were still in danger of being arrested.

Frank was breathless. They all were. There was a sense of panic as they ran hard through the city.

Alongside a canal or river that was not completely iced over, Frank pulled the gun out of his pocket and looked back. They were not being followed. He lobbed the pistol into the water. He just wanted to get back on the ship. He had no need for a gun.

When they recognised the docks ahead of them, they checked again to see if anyone was in pursuit. They seemed to be alone now.

"Should we walk?" Frank asked Joseph.

Joseph didn't reply.

"Good idea," Stephen said. "Just through the docks. Past that guard woman. Let's try and be calm. As far as we know, those three men are the only ones who have a problem with us."

So now the three friends walked, sweating badly under their layers of Arctic clothes, their lungs pumping hard. Frank felt sick from the panic and exhaustion.

Before long they were past the forbidding guards and on their dock, walking up the gangplank and back onboard their ship. HMS *Forgetmenot*. The long grey shape sitting high in the water. The familiar stench of engine oil thick in the air.

Frank began to laugh as soon as they were on board. "That was like the old days," he shouted, adrenaline flushing through his veins. He felt euphoric now the danger was over. Stephen grinned and clapped Frank on the back. But Joseph was standing rigid, staring out to sea, away from Russia, as the Master-at-Arms rushed down the metal steps, eyeing them.

"Right, lads. What was that about? I saw you running from miles off. Come on."

Frank told him everything. The walk. Being followed, arrested. And then the fight. He even owned up about the gun.

The Master-at-Arms frowned, scanned the dock and beyond. "Your shore leave is over," he said. "You'll remain below deck until we are at sea. Got it?"

"Yes, sir."

Joseph had still not spoken.

"Are you all right, son?" the Master-at-Arms asked him, his voice gentler now. "Do you need to go to the sickbay?"

"No, sir. Thank you, sir."

The Master-at-Arms raised an eyebrow, then studied Frank and Stephen again. "Right. Go on then. Get lost. I have to tell the captain about this. Just in case we get any more visitors."

As the Master-at-Arms climbed the ladder back up to the bridge, Frank felt his euphoria dissolve and be replaced by a sudden rush of rage. He was furious with Joseph for putting them all in danger.

"That was all your fault, you know! If we'd not

been lucky and fought our way out of that, we could be on our way to a salt mine now. Or worse. You blew it."

Joseph made no reply.

"Christ!" Frank couldn't ever remember feeling or speaking like this before. He rarely – if ever – lost his temper. "Do you think that because you can speak Russian you are so much better than us? That school really taught you well, didn't it? Accept it, Joe. You caused that whole situation. Can't you even say sorry?"

Before Frank had a chance to say any more, Joseph came at him, punching him on the arm – only missing his head because Frank turned to avoid the blow. Frank then hit Joseph hard in the jaw, catching his friend off balance, and somehow the two boys ended up on the cold wet deck of HMS *Forgetmenot* on their hands and knees.

Then Stephen was between them. "Stand up! Stop." He was speaking in a quiet voice. "You'll be placed on a charge and up before the captain if anyone sees you."

Even without Stephen's warning, the brief fight was over. The two friends were left staring at each other in disbelief. They had come to blows for the first time since they were eight or nine. Looking into Joseph's eyes now, after punching him in the face, Frank felt sadness more than anything else.

He watched his best friend stand.

"You're pathetic," Joseph said, then turned and walked towards the stern of the ship.

Frank felt devastated. The ache in his shoulder and fist were nothing compared to the pain deep down inside.

THE SECOND CONVOY

TWELVE

Kola Inlet, October 1943

The ship's crew assembled on the quarter deck at dawn the next morning. Everyone knew they were heading south, home to Britain with a new convoy, the larger freighters carrying cargoes of timber from the northern Russian forests.

"We are hoping for a quieter run back to Britain," Captain Whitaker said. "A pile of wood is not so interesting to the Germans. They want the aeroplanes and tanks. However ... we do have reports of a wolfpack of U-boats to the south of Bear Island. And also ... well ... there is always the chance

that the enemy will deploy the *Scharnhorst*. We've received notice that it has been spotted in these waters and that they intend to use it."

As they made their way to their posts, Frank could see worry on the faces of the other sailors. The presence of a U-boat wolfpack wasn't great, but it was the other news that had sent a shiver through the crew.

The *Scharnhorst*.

Leading Seaman Bushell had mentioned it on their journey north. The *Scharnhorst* was the most feared German vessel on the ocean. The buzz was that if the *Scharnhorst* caught up with you, you were as good as in the sea, freezing to death, or caught in the darkening bowels of your ship as it plummeted to the seabed.

Frank looked around for Joseph. There was no sign of him. Now more than ever he really wanted to

talk to his friend. But Joseph clearly didn't want to talk to him. Since the row yesterday, Joseph had avoided him, refused to look at him, even turned his back the one time Frank had approached him to talk about it.

He had never had an argument with anyone like that before. Not with his mum. Not with friends. It was all he could think about and he was desperate to make things right between them. Frank was surprised what a devastating effect this fall-out was having on him.

Once they were underway, however, Frank tried to focus on his job: keeping HMS *Forgetmenot* and its convoy safe.

Throughout Frank's first watch on the journey south, the weather was calm. He enjoyed seeing the northern edge of Russia slide by and patches of low sunlight catching the surface of the sea. But however picturesque it was, he was constantly vigilant. They

were only thirty miles from the nearest German airfield on occupied Norwegian land. And U-boats had been known to come this far north.

Soon there was only dark sea. Black waves. So little light that the only shapes he could see were the tips of the waves as they broke white around the ship. But Frank continued to scan from side to side, his binoculars fixed to his brow.

Later that evening the air seemed to change. It was colder and an eerie mist, almost like smoke, seemed to lift off the surface of the waves. Frank knew this was caused by the warm water of the Gulf Stream hitting the frozen air of the Arctic. It was something his grandad had told him about. But the strange mists made his job more difficult. Frank had been trained to search for the shapes of periscopes and mines, but now, in the dark and the mist, he thought he could see faces, heads. Maybe arms flailing in the water.

Frank stopped himself. He had to get a grip. But it was so eerie out here, his mind was playing terrible tricks on him.

Towards the end of his watch, Frank's thoughts turned to Joseph once more, and he wished again that he hadn't lost his temper. The tanker to the side of him released fog buoys to help the ships see each other in the increasingly thick fog, and as Frank stared at them he decided that he would speak to Joseph and sort things out the first chance he got, force him into a conversation. He couldn't bear to go on feeling like this.

Down below deck, however, he couldn't find Joseph at first. The atmosphere on board the ship was claustrophobic and tense as everyone continued to worry about the dual threat of U-boat attacks and the *Scharnhorst*.

Frank queued at the galley for his dinner: minced beef with potatoes and something orange he couldn't

identify. Behind the galley hatch one of the cooks dropped a metal tin that hit the floor with a clang.

Everyone froze. They all knew that there were orders not to slam doors, not to drop mess tins or even to put a metal mug down on the table too firmly. Frank studied his fellow sailors in that moment. They were nervy. And with good reason. In the dark, the submarine periscopes would struggle to find the ships. But their listening devices would be able to hear a loud clang reverberating around a ship's hull, then through the ocean.

Frank made his way to his mess to eat. Some men from his own watch were already sleeping on bunks at the side of the room or in hammocks. He now spotted Joseph sitting reading at one of the tables fixed towards the centre of the room. Stephen was there too but sitting at a different table.

Frank sat with Stephen but said nothing. There

was an uneasy silence in the mess room, broken by the sound of someone down the ship dropping something else. A hammer in the engine room, perhaps?

Frank sat there, occasionally glancing at Joseph. This was killing him. He needed his friend to smile at him or say a few words. Why was it so unbearable to have fallen out with a lifelong friend? What were you supposed to do about it?

"Attention all U-boats," Stephen said in a stage whisper. "Attention. We're over here. This way, please, with your torpedoes. This way, Mr Hitler."

Frank couldn't help but smile. He saw Stephen wink back at him.

"Uncle Joe?" said Stephen, breaking the silence again.

No reply.

"Comrade?"

Still no reply. Just a hand gesture from Joseph.

Stephen rolled his eyes. "Look, Joseph," he said. "We've been friends all our lives. You can't let a fight come between you like this ... Frank was angry about what happened in Murmansk, but he's tried to apologise to you. Please ... this has to stop ... he's doing my head in with his moping. You both are."

Now Joseph stood up, his eyes cast down as he eased himself up into his hammock and turned his back again.

Stephen shrugged. "Night, night then, Uncle Joe."

Frank finished his dinner, took his mess tin to clean it out and climbed into his hammock. Then he stared at the inside of the hull of the ship, the slight curve in the wall of steel between them and the freezing sea, watching for a torpedo to burst through.

Back on deck three hours later, having seen Stephen head down below to the engine room, it was like

sailing on a different sea. The fog had lifted. Without wind, there were no waves, no swell. And the temperature – even high above the North Cape of Norway – was mild to warm. The Gulf Stream again, Frank guessed.

They were still on alert. The lookouts had been reminded that it might look calm out there, but the calmer the conditions, the easier it was for the Germans to attack.

But it was not as likely as they headed south without tanks and aeroplanes. The wolfpacks – as the captain had hopefully suggested – were expected to save their battery power and weaponry for the northbound convoys loaded with military hardware. There was no call for Action Stations.

As a result, men were able to sleep in the four-hour breaks between their watches. In the galley the cooks were able to prepare meals, not just

round after round of corned-beef sandwiches. You could take your time over a cup of kye. Enjoy it, even.

Frank imagined this was how it would feel to be on a cruise in peacetime. He remembered the great white ocean liners that used to sail from Plymouth before the war. To Australia. To America. People travelling across the world by sea. You could just look out at the ocean and search for whales and islands and other friendly ships. That must have been amazing. To be at sea on a pleasure cruise.

Frank snapped out of his pre-war fantasy when he saw it. Another white line. Unmistakable.

"Torpedo! Starboard bow, side-on," Frank shouted to anyone who could hear him.

THIRTEEN

Almost as soon as he called out "Torpedo", Frank felt HMS *Forgetmenot* begin a sharp evasive turn. A move, like last time, to avoid the attack incoming from a U-boat.

The ship reared up, shuddering, then crashed down again as a colossal wave broke over it, showering men as they grabbed for guard rails and lifelines. Frank was soaked and freezing. He gasped for air.

Where did that wave come from? his mind asked, not understanding what had happened. Not yet. Too much was happening at once. It was impossible to work out what was going on.

Still confused, Frank looked around hoping to catch the eye of another sailor to check that everything was all right, and noticed, to his horror, that the mast of HMS *Forgetmenot* above the bridge was at an angle of thirty degrees and the captain was staggering up a sloped deck to reach the tubes.

Now Frank knew what was happening – they had been hit.

Even so, he kept his eyes on the captain, waiting for confirmation and instructions about what to do next.

"Open the drenching gear." The order came from the captain.

Frank felt a sharp sudden acidic sting in his throat, then his mouth filled with vomit.

Stephen.

Drenching gear.

He thought of Stephen in his boiler suit. In the

warmth of the engine room. He remembered clearly what his friend had told him about the eighth way to die.

The seven men working the engine room would have about a minute, Frank knew, to endure freezing water that would now be closing in around them. With the hatches and doors sealed shut, the sea would lift them off their feet and they would tread water, still hoping for a miracle. Their heads would hit the ceiling, the water still rising. Cold. Monstrous. All fires in the engine room would be extinguished. As would the lives of the men in there. Of Stephen.

The ship shuddered. Frank felt the explosion at the same time as he saw it: a blinding red flash from behind him projected onto the waves.

Had they been hit again? Had some of the missile stores exploded? He heard the sound of feet in corridors, on ladders. Shouting. Screaming. Chaos.

But still the captain was at his post, listening to a message coming to him through the tubes.

Frank saw him nod and tighten his life jacket. Frank did the same to his.

"Man the life rafts," the captain shouted. "Abandon ship."

An alarm was wailing from one of the ships to the starboard side. It was hard to hear it above the buzzing in Frank's ears.

Aldis lamps flashed across the dark waves and the air filled with the brutal stench of oil. A star shell from another ship flooded them with light, revealing thick black smoke fogging everything.

HMS *Forgetmenot* was sinking. Actually sinking. Frank could see the flames and feel searing heat around him. He knew that it was likely the whole ship could go up in a vast explosion and so he did the only thing he could. He ran to the side of the

ship and – unable to see a life raft within reach on deck or in the water – he jumped over the guard rail and tumbled into the churning, thrashing waves beneath him.

Frank was in the air for one, maybe two, seconds. Then smack! He was freezing cold. Gasping for air, he went under, managing to hold his breath so as not to take in any water.

Frank knew that he *had* to get away from the ship. Every sailor understood that if you were caught in the wake of the ship, it could pull you along the hull, then take you down, under the stern to the waiting propellers to be turned into mince.

Restrained by his heavy clothes, Frank struggled to swim in the direction he thought was away from HMS *Forgetmenot*. He could see very little. But then, as a wave lifted him, he found himself so high on a swell that he could identify the hulls of ships, hear

sirens roaring across the water. Then he was plunged down again, into the darkness of a trough, and Frank stared up around him, trying to make sure he was not in the path of a freighter. He remembered to activate the red light on his life jacket. It would help him be spotted. If anyone was looking.

That was when he saw the star. Just fleetingly. The Arctic Star. The star Joseph had pointed out to him what seemed like a lifetime ago as they sailed north.

Frank began swimming again. No time to think. He couldn't stop to gaze at the stars – he'd be dead in seconds. He sensed his lungs and heart and legs becoming colder and colder. He had to keep moving, find a way to survive each crater of foaming water that he was plunged into.

But what was he swimming to? Would any other ship pick him up?

And then Frank saw a life jacket high on the

swell above him, its red light flickering. Another man, his head tipped back, perhaps unconscious. Frank scrambled through the water towards him. Someone else had made it off HMS *Forgetmenot*.

He gave it everything. All his strength. But it was so hard to swim now. The cold made his legs ache like they'd been drained of blood. His arms too. And his clothes were feeling heavier and heavier, his lungs burning as if he was climbing a mountain.

When he reached the other man, he found him now face down in the water.

Frank turned him over.

Joseph.

It was Joseph!

Frank lifted Joseph's head out of the water and turned him onto his back.

"Wake up," he shouted, trying to make Joseph hear him above the roar and thrashing of the waves.

Ships passed either side of them. Huge dark hulls blacking out the starlight. Frank could feel the churning of propellers, the water moving.

It was cold. So cold. His teeth were chattering. His breathing shallow.

Frank punched Joseph and shouted at him to wake up as a great thud reverberated through the water.

Depth charges.

Other Royal Navy ships were catapulting depth charges into the sea to warn off submarines or even sink them. A depth charge might blow up near them and rupture all their internal organs. It was another way to die. One that Stephen had not thought of. But Frank knew he had to think of ways of staying alive, not of dying.

Frank turned Joseph to keep his face from the water again. His friend had not responded yet. He

wanted to get him out of the water. He gazed around him to see what was left of the convoy. Most of the ships had passed them now.

Tankers. Freighters. Cruisers. Corvettes. All of them under orders not to stop and pick up survivors. Maybe Frank and Joseph had been spotted from those passing decks. But there was only one ship in each column of the convoy that could stop and pick them up.

The rescue ship.

And here it was at the back of the convoy. Smaller than the freighters and cruisers. If the rescue ship missed Frank and Joseph, that would be it. All they would be able to do was watch the convoy lumber south. Then die.

Frank lifted his head up and called out, tried to manoeuvre the red light on Joseph's life jacket so it could be seen from the rescue ship. But as it began

to pass them, its hull so close they could almost touch it, Frank saw no sign that they had been spotted. And he felt even more conscious of the black empty waves behind this last vessel of their convoy.

This last chance.

Then, just as the hull of the last ship pushed the sea out of its way, lifting Frank and Joseph in its wake, Frank felt something hit him on the head. Reeling, blinded by water and confusion, he reached out his free arm, the one not holding on to Joseph, and his hand closed around something.

A rope.

And there was more. A net. What was this? He didn't have time to think. Frank's one hope was that this rope, this net, was a scramble net, thrown down by the men on the rescue ship to pick up any survivors.

"Joseph," he gasped. "Come on. We're safe."

But now – with the net to hold onto and with air to breathe – Frank could see his friend's face properly for the first time.

He was pale. Blue-lipped.

His eyes were staring wide at the stars, his mouth gaping open.

Ice was forming on his eyebrows, his hair.

Joseph was dead.

SURVIVOR'S LEAVE

FOURTEEN

As the train thundered through the south-west of England – ploughing past fields and landscapes that seemed so familiar – Frank felt himself trembling. If it wasn't his hands, it was his legs. There were even tremors in his neck.

But it was warm in the small six-seater cabin, stuffy with the windows closed and the late autumn sun blazing in. Frank wasn't trembling because he was cold. It wasn't that. He hadn't been able to stop shaking since the torpedo had hit HMS *Forgetmenot*.

It was a relief to be back on dry land. He looked

out at the hills and fields and towns and realised how much he'd missed the landscapes of England. Even though it was winter, there was so much greenery, so much variety. It was a welcome change from the grey skies and seas of the Arctic.

Passing through Dawlish, Frank saw the coastline. He turned away and looked at the only other passenger in his compartment now that the four American soldiers they had shared it with had alighted at Exeter.

A sailor. Pale-faced. Humourless. Eyes cast down.

Stephen.

Neither of them knew how Stephen had survived. When HMS *Forgetmenot* had been hit by the torpedo, Stephen had been sealed in with the other half-dozen men in the engine room as the drenching gear was opened. But after Frank was

hauled in by the rescue ship, he found Stephen in the galley, where he had been taken to recover.

"How?" Frank had asked when their eyes met.

Stephen shrugged but had no words, no dark humour to make them both laugh.

And that was it. They'd not spoken of any of it since. Neither of them wanted to go over what had happened.

After the train from Edinburgh to London, they had changed to head west to Plymouth, where the four American soldiers had tried to start a conversation. The quartet were young men abroad, undaunted by fear and full of the excitement of a weekend's leave in London and the fun they'd had.

Stephen had just closed his eyes and pretended to be asleep. Frank talked to them for a while. Then – feeling shattered – he told the Americans the truth. They were on survivor's leave. They'd been

torpedoed. In the Arctic. They were the only two survivors out of eighty-five. Their best friend had been killed. His name was Joseph.

As the train drew into Plymouth, Frank could still feel himself trembling.

"Shall we walk?" Stephen suggested once they had alighted.

Frank nodded. It was three miles home, but Frank knew that Stephen would prefer to avoid a tram or a bus. Why cram yourself into a small space with other people with the doors closed? The train had been bad enough.

The sun was shining as they made their way down the hill, the city centre busy. Delivery lorries and trams, bicycles weaving along the roads. Frank found it quite bizarre to see groups and pairs of people chatting and laughing, and vehicles moving

around the broken city. Even though the city had been bombed before he'd left, the sight of all the collapsed masonry and damaged buildings still felt shocking. Plymouth had been left in ruins by German bombs.

But still, in the gardens running down into town, he saw women watching children at play, running round and round, laughing. The women smiling too. One caught his gaze and her eyes lingered on him. Frank had no idea how to react, so he just looked away.

That was when he saw Joseph.

Stocky. Dark-haired. Upright posture, with his head back. It had to be him.

"Joseph!" Frank called out. "Joseph!"

But the dark-haired man did not turn round and Frank felt Stephen's hand on his shoulder.

"You all right?" Stephen asked.

"It's Joseph. There must have been another rescue ship," gasped Frank.

"It's not Joseph."

Frank wanted to pull away from Stephen, prove that he was right. Then he understood what his friend was saying. Joseph couldn't be alive. The only chance he would have had was being picked up by the rescue ship. And Frank had seen him drift behind it when he'd climbed the scramble net.

"I thought it was him," Frank mumbled.

Stephen shrugged. That was all he seemed to do now. Shrug.

"It wasn't him, was it?" Frank asked again.

Stephen shook his head. They walked in silence for several minutes until Stephen spoke.

"We should go to see his dad," he said.

"We should." Frank felt a shudder of fear. "But let's leave it a day or two."

"Yes."

They walked on. Over to the other side of town to where they could smell the sea over the stench of countless buildings ruined by the Blitz.

Neither of them had suggested that they divert via Plymouth Hoe, but, without a word, it was what they did.

Up the hill, past the elegant houses on the right and alongside the park to the left, and then over the back of the hill to see Plymouth Sound and Drake's Island squatting low in the water.

The sea. But not any old sea. Not a sea wild with anger, frozen by Arctic winds. This was *their* sea. This was home.

Now they turned towards Devonport, their own part of the city. To where Frank's mum and Stephen's parents were waiting for them. They'd sent a telegram to let them know.

FIFTEEN

They picked up their pace as they walked from Plymouth Hoe, through Stonehouse and on to Devonport.

The streets appeared the same as they always had. Terraced houses. Churches. Schools. The butcher's. The baker's. That was until you looked a little closer and saw tape across windows to stop the glass shattering if a bomb hit. Until you noticed that the majority of vehicles on the roads were not private or commercial but military. Like Murmansk.

Closer to home now, they passed their old school, which looked smaller than it had the last

time Frank had walked past it, even though he'd only been away from home for a matter of weeks. It was a relief to see every house on their street was intact. No bomb damage.

The first house they came to on the corner was Joseph's. Frank must have gone to the front door a thousand times to ask if Joseph was playing out. More than a thousand, probably.

But he'd never do it again.

There were no lights on in Joseph's house and Frank wondered if Joseph's dad had gone away after receiving the news.

The realisation that Joseph was dead hit Frank like one of the giant waves they'd suffered in the Arctic. Here was his house. The house where he would usually be, if he wasn't out with Frank and Stephen. But Joseph wasn't there. He was somewhere in that frozen sea.

Frank's thoughts failed him. He felt numb.

The two sailors glanced at each other. Neither had anything to say. Nor did they want to hear anything. It was clear they had both been pitched again into grief for their lost friend.

They parted and Frank walked on. He lived at the far end of the road. A few metres further on. He stepped up his pace.

Then he saw his house. The trellis round the door. A rose tree but no flowers this late in the year. The window frames smartly painted by his mum. No house on the street was better looked after.

Frank heard the clang of a crane echoing from across the docks and glanced down the hill. The clang was an echo of Murmansk that he put to the back of his mind. He didn't want to remember Russia.

Now doors and windows opened.

"Welcome home, son." Mrs Nunn from over the

road was standing in her doorway. "Your mum will be so glad to see you. You look so handsome in your uniform."

"Thank you, Mrs Nunn."

Now Mr Knowles put his head out of the window of another house.

"Good to see you, son," he called.

"I hope yours are all well?" Frank asked both neighbours.

Mrs Nunn and Mr Knowles both said they were. Frank reflected that between them the two neighbours had six children – two girls and four boys – all in the Navy or Army or land forces. So this was what homecoming was like, he thought. You say hello to your neighbours first, then ask if their children are still alive.

He stood at his front door, then knocked and waited for his mum to answer it.

She emerged wearing a smile and carrying a rabbit.

After a hug, she took his kitbag and handed him the rabbit.

"You know what to do," she said.

SIXTEEN

They had the rabbit for dinner. Skinned, boned and chopped up, with potatoes and carrots. They ate in the small dark kitchen overlooking a square garden, half of it given over to a vegetable plot, the other half an enclosure with five or six more rabbits lolloping about. Frank's mind drifted: did the surviving rabbits think about the one he was eating now? Did they grieve?

Frank had noticed that there was a letter addressed to him on the mantlepiece. He didn't mention it. But he knew what it was. Orders from the Royal Navy about where he was to report next.

His next posting. His next ship. His next nightmare.

Now he was at home, he couldn't imagine going back to sea, couldn't imagine being back on board a ship, waiting for the next attack. Could he refuse to go back? Reject his family's proud naval history?

He wanted to talk to his mum about it. She was the only one he could speak to about the way he was feeling. But he was surprised to realise that things felt tense between them. They were talking, but not really saying anything.

When Frank had imagined coming home, he had thought that he and his mum would slip into their usual comfortable relationship, chatting and laughing as normal. But somehow it wasn't like that.

"This meat is good," he said to stop his train of thought.

Frank's mum smiled. "A fair bit fresher than

the meat you'd get from the galley," she said, looking away into the garden when his hand began to shake.

After they'd eaten, Frank and his mum shared a bottle of her home-brewed beer in the back garden as the sky faded from grey to black. All the lights in the house were off. All the lights up the road, in fact. In case the Luftwaffe decided to pay Plymouth another visit. Thanks to the blackout, the stars were impressive even in the city.

"Is Joseph's dad at home?" Frank asked.

Mum nodded. "But we don't see much of him." She paused. "Will you go and see him?"

Now it was Frank's turn to hesitate. He shrugged. "I will. Maybe not tomorrow."

"Go as soon as you can, eh?"

"I will."

Frank had not spoken about what had happened when HMS *Forgetmenot* went down, nor what had

happened to Joseph. He didn't want to now he was home. And his mum had not asked.

"And when do you have to go back?" she said now. "Seeing as we're talking about things like that. You had that letter this morning. What ship are you on?"

Frank looked at his mum. "You tell me," he said. "I'm sure you'll have read it?"

Mum laughed. "So you don't mind that I peeked?"

Frank shrugged. "It doesn't matter. What does it say?"

"You have eleven days. Then you have to report to HMS *Belfast* in Scotland."

Frank nodded. "The *Belfast*. Big ship, that. A cruiser."

"And a lucky ship." Mum looked serious.

"Is it?"

"'It hit a magnetic mine in the Firth of Forth a few years ago. Had a complete refit. Rumours are

it had its refit here in Plymouth. And it has all the modern technology."

Frank was amused that his mum still knew so much about the Navy. And that she knew about HMS *Belfast* coming here, like he did. Now his eyes fixed on the Arctic Star.

"See that star?" Frank asked.

"The North Star?" Mum said.

"Yeah. Me and Joseph ... we called it the Arctic Star. We'd look at it when we were on the ship."

Mum nodded but said nothing.

"I don't believe in it any more," Frank said suddenly, shocked now he had said out loud the thoughts that had been overwhelming him.

"Believe in what?" Mum asked calmly. "The star?"

"The Navy."

Another silence. Frank wasn't sure how his mum would take this. Tell him he was a coward? Beg

him to run away and hide until the end of the war? What does a Navy mum say to a sailor who is scared to death?

"I don't want to go back," he added.

There. He'd said to his mum what he and Stephen had not dared say to each other.

Mum said nothing still.

Frank felt irritated. "So what are you going to tell me to do?" he snapped.

Mum let out a short laugh.

"Is it funny?" Frank stood for a moment. Then sat, apologised for being rude. He waited for his mum to say what she had to say.

"I have no doubt," she said at last, carefully weighing her words, "that you will regret it if you do go back and that you will regret it if you don't. Both options are unthinkable. You have to decide what you want to live with for the rest of your life."

Frank nodded. She made a good point.

Frank slept in his old familiar bedroom. He leaned his kitbag against the wall under the window.

The bed was small, built for when Frank was a child, but it beat sleeping in a hammock. It took him a while to get to sleep properly, because every time he closed his eyes and began to drift off, he would open them to imagine a torpedo blasting through the wall of the house, followed by gallons and gallons of freezing seawater.

Then he would have to find a way to stop himself shaking.

Frank woke for a final time before dawn, soaking wet. Night sweats. Very quickly he became cold. He had a choice. Put some of his Arctic kit on to stay warm or go downstairs and start a fire, make a cup of tea.

Frank chose the fire.

Drinking his tea, he cast his eyes around the front room. The photographs on the wall seemed to be staring at him. His dad, grandad, uncles, all in Navy uniforms. And a new picture he had not noticed the night before.

Him. Frank.

In his uniform. Staring back at him like all the others.

When Mum came downstairs at seven o'clock, she found Frank leafing through the sketchbook he had inherited. He had a half-smile on his lips as he looked at his and his father's drawings.

"I'm going to see Joseph's dad later," he told her. "I'll take Stephen."

"Good lad," Mum said. "Give him something good to remember Joseph by."

"What do you mean?" Frank asked. "I don't have anything of his."

"No, I don't mean that ..." she said. "I mean whatever you tell him about Joseph will be his last memory of the boy, his son."

Frank's dread of going to see his friend's dad grew even stronger. But he knew he had to do it. He would have wanted Joseph to do the same for him.

SEVENTEEN

It was only a five-minute walk to Joseph's house. Frank put on his uniform and suggested Stephen do the same. His mum had told him they had to show respect.

Rain clouds were billowing in from the sea as they approached the door.

"What do we say?" Stephen put his hand out to stop Frank knocking.

"I don't know," Frank said. "What would your dad want to hear about you if I turned up on your doorstep?"

Stephen shrugged and Frank knocked.

Joseph's dad opened the door, stared at them without comment for a couple of seconds, then stood aside to let them in.

They were shown through to the front room. Joseph's dad switched the light on. It was the only light on in the house.

"Trying to save money," he remarked. It was the first thing he had said to them.

There was a photograph of Joseph in a wooden frame on the fireplace. No fire burning in the hearth. The room was cold. Frank could see his own breath, the temperature was that low.

"Please sit down."

The room was small. Floral wallpaper. Net curtains that blocked out half the winter light. They could hear rain on the windowpanes. The clouds were overhead now, darkening the sky.

"Tea?"

"Yes, please."

Frank and Stephen were left in the front room for ten minutes, listening to the sound of crockery and cutlery clinking through the door, a kettle screaming, then a long silence when nothing seemed to be happening in the kitchen. They studied the photograph of Joseph. He was trying to smile. Frank stared at the picture and shook his head. He closed his eyes, trying not to get upset. Then he opened them and sighed.

He noticed Stephen was watching him.

"I don't envy you that row you had with him," Stephen said. "You can never talk it out, make it better. But don't let it stop you remembering eighteen years of friendship. The three of us. You have to find a way to focus on that, Frank."

Frank nodded, but all he could hear from Stephen was words. They couldn't change the guilt

he felt about how things had been left between him and Joseph.

Joseph's dad came in with a tray. A teapot, milk jug, three cups.

"We're sorry about Joseph," Stephen said.

"Thanks, lads," he said. His skin was grey, except for around his eyes, where it was red. In fact, his eyes were red too. Bloodshot.

Frank had no idea what to say to this man – a widower – who had just lost his son and now had no one.

They sipped their tea in silence until Joseph's dad broke it.

"I wonder if this is more difficult for you than me, lads. You'll be thinking, *What the hell do I say to this man?* I'll help you out. How was he? In himself? You know? The days before."

Frank remembered his mum's advice. Choose

something good to tell Joseph's dad. Something he can hang on to. And Frank did not want to mention the argument they had had, the disagreement that they never got the chance to resolve. Why curse Joseph's dad with those thoughts? It was enough that Frank had to deal with them himself.

"He ... erm ... well, one of his dreams came true," Frank stuttered.

Joseph's dad sat forward. "Go on."

Frank could feel Stephen watching him as well as the older man.

"He got to visit Russia."

"Oh, he did? That's wonderful. Did he speak to anyone? Did he use his Russian? He spent a lot of time on his learning at that school."

Frank felt surprised by a rush of pleasure. "He did," Frank replied. "He spoke to a guard. A woman selling roasted food. Some policemen. And other

people around the docks. We were very impressed, weren't we, Stephen?"

"Very," Stephen said.

The three men laughed gently together as they talked about the boys' hour in Murmansk. Frank held back the stuff about the secret police, the fight and running for their lives. Joseph's dad didn't need to know that.

Then there was another silence. Before Joseph's dad hit them with a question. "Can I ask a favour?"

"Of course. Anything," said Frank.

"Can you tell me what happened? Exactly what happened to Joe? How he died, I mean. I'd like to know."

Stephen looked at Frank. His eyes huge. Frank could tell Stephen didn't fancy answering this one either.

Joseph's dad went on, his voice urgent. "You

understand it will help me. He was my son. The Navy sent me a message. You know. The usual thing. *Your son died serving his country, blah, blah …* and I know that. I understand that. They have to make it sound heroic. But for me, I am more concerned with the facts."

Frank nodded.

"I am his dad," the older man went on. "A dad wants to know what happened to his son. If I know the details, I won't need to imagine worse."

Frank leaned forward. He would do what he was asked. He would say exactly what happened. For Joseph's dad. For Joseph. He knew that his friend would want him to do this for him.

"When the torpedo hit," Frank began, "Joseph was on lookout on the top deck. I didn't see him between us being hit and me going in the water. I found him in the sea a minute or two later. He wasn't wounded. All

I can imagine is that he was either thrown into the water when the torpedo struck or he jumped when the captain told us to abandon ship, like I did. He had a life jacket on, so maybe the latter. I don't know.

"I am pretty sure he would have been alive when he went overboard. But he could have broken his neck when he hit the water – that can happen if you have a life jacket on. So he probably didn't drown. I would have thought he froze to death or broke his neck. That it took less than five minutes."

Frank didn't want Joseph's dad to ask him what happened when the rescue ship arrived. But it was likely he would want to know.

He coughed. He'd just tell him. Get it over with.

"When the rescue ship arrived … I knew he was dead and I couldn't get him up the scramble net. I had to leave him in the water to save myself. But he was dead. I'm sorry."

Joseph's dad stood up and put his hand on Frank's shoulder. "Don't apologise, son. You did what you could and here you are now doing more. You've told me what I wanted to know. That must have been tough. You were always a great friend to my lad. Both of you were. I won't forget that. And Joseph knew it too."

Frank couldn't reply. A wave of emotion hit him hard and he stared at the floor to avoid showing it.

"We were proud to have him as a friend," Stephen said for both of them.

Outside, it was raining hard now and it was cold. Frank and Stephen headed back to Frank's mum's.

As they walked, the wind whipping around the buildings, stripping the last leaves of autumn off the trees, Frank stopped, allowing the rain to soak him. He had never felt so exhausted. Not even after he'd been in the sea. Or after the fight.

"When I saw the papers and the letter telling me about my next posting last night on the mantelpiece at home, I decided I was going to pack it in," he told Stephen. "Run away. Hide. I don't know."

Stephen laughed. "I think that's normal. And now?"

"I'll go back," Frank replied. "We don't have much choice, do we?"

The rain intensified. But it was nothing compared to the weather they'd endured in the Arctic.

"Not much," Stephen said. "We might as well fool ourselves we're desperate to get back at the Germans. At least we'll fool everyone else."

The pair smiled.

"I'm on the *Belfast*," Frank said. "Did you get a letter?"

"I did, mate. HMS *Belfast* for me too, leaving for Murmansk in ten days' time."

THE THIRD CONVOY

EIGHTEEN

Loch Ewe, December 1943

Three cruisers steamed out of Loch Ewe in the north of Scotland at 1300 hours on 12 December 1943. Two weeks before Christmas.

HMS *Sheffield*.

HMS *Norfolk*.

HMS *Belfast*.

Their mission: to meet up with Arctic Convoys in the High Arctic and escort them through U-boat infested waters.

Frank and Stephen stood on the starboard side of HMS *Belfast* as they slipped out into the Minch,

the body of wild water that lay between the Scottish mainland and the Western Isles.

From the high deck, they saw low barren hills in shades of grey and brown, obscured much of the time by a swirling mist. Scotland slid out of view as the seas built around them and the fog thickened. Then they turned their backs on the nothingness and admired their new ship.

To be part of the crew on a cruiser was utterly different to being on a corvette. HMS *Belfast* was nearly two hundred metres long and had a crew of nine hundred and fifty, not eighty-five. It was enormous. Vast. Colossal. There were no words big enough to describe its size.

It was winter. The sea was wild even before HMS *Belfast* hit the open water. Great waves and howling winds. They ploughed on as the hollow booms of the waves collapsing on themselves echoed

off the ship's hull. Frank shivered in the icy blasting wind. If it was this cold and wild off Scotland, what would conditions be like in the Arctic?

Dark, he guessed, with the sun not coming up at all now it was winter. Fifty-foot waves day after day, tossing the ship side to side, down and up.

But Frank knew that he must hope for storms. Fear of the weather was easy to manage – you could see it coming. Predict it. The stormier the better. Then those other fears would not come into play. The ones about what was deep down in the dark waters or high in the skies above.

U-boats waiting to send them to their deaths.

Line after line of bombers swooping down on them.

If the seas were calm, that was what they should expect. And, anyway, Frank already understood that high seas made less impact on a

huge ship like the *Belfast*. The waves barely moved the deck up and down.

But while they perhaps did not have to fear the weather as much onboard this vast fighting ship, they did still have to fear the *Scharnhorst*. The captain had told them as much before they cast off.

The *Scharnhorst* – the monster ship that Hitler had sent to cut off the Arctic Convoys for good – was waiting in the fjords of Norway to attack. And this time they were expecting it to be deployed.

"Lightning doesn't strike the same place twice," Frank said to Stephen.

"Meaning?" Stephen asked.

"Meaning we can't be hit by a torpedo again. We've already had that. Have you ever met any sailor who's been torpedoed twice?"

Stephen looked at Frank and shook his head. "Are you mad?" he said, a slight twinkle in his eyes.

"You can't meet them when they're all at the bottom of the sea."

Frank laughed. It was Stephen's first attempt at a joke in over a month. He was glad of it.

The hardest aspect of being aboard the *Belfast* – for Frank – was sleeping below deck in his hammock in the mess. How could he rest, let alone sleep, when he was constantly remembering the night of the torpedo?

On some ships, men who had been torpedoed had been known to sleep up on the deck in falling snow rather than face a night below. One comfort for Frank was that he knew he could be in the open air – from hammock to deck – in fifteen seconds.

He'd practised.

His other comfort was the ship's cat.

There hadn't been a mouser on the *Forgetmenot*, but HMS *Belfast* had Frankenstein. The cat.

As luck would have it, most mice on board
the ship seemed to pass along Frank and Stephen's
mess deck, probably because of the heat and food
smells coming from the galley. This meant that in
their down time the men could watch a daily battle
between cat and mouse.

While they were in London – passing through
en route for Scotland – Frank and Stephen had
gone to the cinema. They watched news films about
how the Allies were gearing up to defeat the Nazis.
Frank drank it in. Images of Winston Churchill with
world leaders, soldiers, sailors and airmen, planning
for victory.

There were cartoons too. Their favourite was a
new one called *Tom and Jerry*, about a cat that was
trying to catch and kill a mouse that could never
be caught. Now on the *Belfast* they could watch
cat-and-mouse games being played out in real life.

Once Frankenstein was at Action Stations and the mouse had been sighted skittering along the bulkheads, darting from corner to corner, ledge to ledge, all the men knew how it would end. But it was still fun to watch.

They took bets on how long it would take and how many pieces of mouse would be left over for them to clean up. Just a tail? Maybe a head? Or nothing.

After the hunt, the ship's cat would parade in front of the men as if she wanted applause, then she would climb into her own small cat hammock, set up by the crew for her comfort.

The cat made Frank feel better. For a while. It was an entertainment, something to take his mind off what was coming. The same way a cinema full of people watching cartoons could be distracted from the Blitz.

On the night watches during the two weeks it took

them to reach Russia, Frank would sometimes glance at the sky, seeking out the Arctic Star.

When he found it – on the nights there were no clouds – he would first think about Joseph and remember his dad's words.

You were always a great friend to my lad.

Then Frank would think about his mum at home with the ongoing threat from German bombers. He hated the thought of his mum alone at the mercy of the Luftwaffe. But it helped him too. It reminded him why he was here, enduring this; it reminded him what the war was for.

NINETEEN

Barents Sea, Christmas Day, 1943

And then it was Christmas Day. The first one Frank
would spend without his mum.

It didn't feel great and he knew she'd be missing
him too, on her own at home. But he tried to comfort
himself with the thought that surely the war would
be over by next Christmas – if they did what they
had to do. Surely next year he and his mum would
be together again to celebrate. You had to think like
that during wartime.

Christmas dinner on the Arctic Ocean was
a bully-beef sandwich and some dried biscuits.

Conditions were too rough for a proper feed. But they'd been promised a real Christmas dinner once the seas were quiet. And – although he fancied some turkey – Frank was always happier when the seas were wild.

HMS *Belfast* and its two sister cruisers were heading south now, having seen one convoy safely into Murmansk but not docking themselves as they had to meet up with and shield the next convoy that was on its way north.

The ship was at second degree of readiness, one level below Action Stations. They knew something was coming. Danger. Conflict. War.

But not yet. For now they needed to rest. And be ready for that something. Christmas Day or not.

An hour to go until the late afternoon watch began, there was a crackle on the tubes and the captain's voice sounded.

Some of the men were already on their feet. Was it time? Frank asked himself. Was this it? Action Stations?

The captain began by wishing them a Merry Christmas, then he asked them to join him in listening to the King's Christmas message that he was going to relay to them live from home by radio.

As the national anthem crackled over the ship's broadcast system, Frank stood, as he had always been told to. Several men joined in, singing in low voices, looking at their feet or hands.

Then, after the music faded, the King's Christmas 1943 message began, his voice faltering, hesitating before going on:

And once again, from our home in England, the Queen and I send our Christmas greetings and good wishes to each one of you all the world over.

Some of you may hear me on board your ships, in your aircraft, or as you wait for battle in the jungles of the Pacific Islands, along the Italian Peaks …

To many of you, my words will come as you sit in the quiet of your homes. But, wherever you may be, today of all days in the year, your thoughts will be in distant places and your hearts with those you love.

I hope that my words spoken to them and to you may be the bond that joins us all in one company for a few moments on this Christmas Day …

After the speech, men turned to each other and shook hands. But none spoke.

Frank felt shattered but energised too. He was thinking about his mum. At home. Alone. Listening to the speech on the wireless. He knew she would be

thinking of him listening to the speech too.

In the quiet below decks, from one, two, then several places on the ship, they heard singing floating up corridors and down ladders.

Hark! The herald angels sing,
"Glory to the new-born king!
Peace on earth and mercy mild
God and sinners reconciled."

Christmas Day 1943, as HMS *Belfast* ploughed on through the waves. And Stephen added to the hymn with an extra verse.

Hark! The herald angels sing,
"Glory to the new-born king!
Peace on earth, but not on water.
Scharnhorst, Belfast might have caught yer."

Several sailors laughed at Stephen's song. Frank was glad his friend was cracking jokes again. It was a good sign.

They were all thinking about the *Scharnhorst*. Every man on the ship. But few mentioned it. It lay beneath the surface of every conversation and gesture, like a U-boat biding its time.

Frank was pleased that Stephen could bring it up. Wrapped in a joke or a song. Why not make fun of the fear that was coming your way? Surely the fear would be easier to handle if you'd laughed at it first?

TWENTY

The North Cape, Boxing Day, 1943

Frank and Stephen were off watch and in the mess deck eating breakfast at 0755 hours on Boxing Day when the announcement came. The captain over the tubes.

Men got to their feet. Like last time.

And with good reason.

The captain explained that he had received an intelligence report from Norway, via Britain. The *Scharnhorst* was on the move. The German battleship was coming out to engage with the next Arctic Convoy.

Frank put down his corned-beef sandwich as he felt HMS *Belfast* change its course, turning, maybe even accelerating, as if to begin the charge into battle.

His appetite was gone. He felt his throat seal up like the hatches on the ship were being sealed right now.

This was it.

Stephen stood up and pulled a face just as the ship's alarm went off to indicate Action Stations. Calm and orderly, tight smiles on their faces, Frank and Stephen prepared to leave the mess room.

Before they parted, Stephen put his hand on Frank's shoulder. "Listen," he said. "I've been thinking about Joseph. How cross he was with us."

"Me too," Frank scowled. "Every day. Every hour."

"It was just one of those stupid arguments that friends have. You know that, don't you? Good friends

have rows like that. You have them. You get over them. Really, they only happen to people who care a lot about each other. We were just unlucky that was our last conversation."

Frank nodded.

"And he thought the world of you," Stephen said. "You have to remember that."

Frank nodded again. But said nothing. He knew that Stephen was right, that he just had to remember his lifetime friendship with Joseph, not their last unfortunate conversation.

"But I don't think the world of you," Stephen added. "So when we've been sunk and I'm dead and you're on the rescue ship, don't forget I think you're a clown."

The two friends parted for Action Stations, both of them laughing so hard they had tears in their eyes as one headed up to the main deck, the other

below, to take part in one of the most important and dangerous sea battles of the Second World War.

Frank's post was towards the bow of the ship, on the starboard side. He settled in, binoculars already scanning the sea.

Another crackle on the tubes.

It was the chaplain of the ship this time, his voice slow and calm.

"Now we know we're in for it," another sailor joked loudly across the aft of the ship. "A chat to prepare us for the afterlife? They'll be bringing the rum round soon."

The padre spoke about God.

He spoke about country.

He spoke about sacrifice.

Then he finished with a prayer:

Our Father, who art in heaven

Hallowed be thy name

Thy kingdom come …

After the chaplain spoke, rum was brought to every man. Frank couldn't help chuckling at the comment made earlier. Stephen would have enjoyed the joke.

But the feeling didn't last long.

In bleak, tense silence, without the comforting words of the chaplain echoing off the deck, Frank stared out into the void, scanning the horizon for the first sighting of the *Scharnhorst* but also checking squares of dark sea for U-boats. To his side he could see the silhouetted shape of HMS *Norfolk* a mile away from them. And beyond that he knew HMS *Sheffield* was with them too.

Three cruisers heading to harass the formidable *Scharnhorst*, separating from the

convoy now, taking the fight to the enemy before it annihilated the dozens of merchant ships steaming north.

It felt good to have other Royal Navy ships with them. There was safety in numbers. Imagine being alone in HMS *Belfast* against the far superior *Scharnhorst*. That would be unthinkable. That would surely be the end. But there were three cruisers heading into battle. With three they had a chance.

Time passed.

Nothing for half an hour.

Then an hour had passed.

Ninety minutes.

Frank was beginning to wonder if the battle would ever start, when suddenly a star shell exploded above them, lighting up the whole sky, forcing men used to scanning darkness to cover their eyes.

"Gentlemen," the captain announced over the tubes, "we are about to engage the *Scharnhorst*. Be ready and know that the prayers of our nation and families are with you tonight."

TWENTY-ONE

The star shell sent up to illuminate the theatre of war revealed what looked to Frank like a distant city. But there was no city in the middle of the North Cape in the Arctic Ocean.

Frank knew he was looking at the *Scharnhorst*.

And then suddenly he was thrown forward, his face smashing on the guard rail, the metallic taste of blood in his mouth. His ears were thudding as the air imploded around him. Instinctively he put his hands over them to protect himself from the boom that came like a punch to both ears at once.

What now? What was going on? Were they under attack so soon?

It was unclear. Frank was confused.

Until he heard cheering. And more explosions. Then the prickly, smoky smell of cordite told him what he needed to know: all the guns on HMS *Belfast*'s port side had been fired at the *Scharnhorst*.

Frank's first ever broadside.

More light filled the horizon now as the *Belfast*'s ordnance rained down on its target. The *Scharnhorst* was lit in silhouette, just a few miles away, but Frank could see it changing shape, narrowing, and he knew what that meant.

"*Scharnhorst* turning to head north," Frank reported.

And it was. He could see it with his own eyes. The German battleship was gradually turning, attempting to evade the onslaught.

Was that it? thought Frank. *Was that the extent of the battle?* After the surge of adrenaline he'd experienced following the broadside, he felt a sinking feeling, a sense of disappointment, and realised that he wanted war, wanted conflict. He wanted to see the floating city hit by shells, not for it to sail away again. He wanted to see it burning, exploding, sinking.

For a moment he waited, silently urging the captain of the *Belfast* to go after the *Scharnhorst*, and soon he felt the engine vibrations increase, sensed his ship was turning north. He could see that the *Sheffield* and *Norfolk* were doing the same.

They were going in pursuit of the enemy.

After an hour of the pursuit – all men still at their posts – an Action-Stations dinner was served. Hot soup, meat pie, jam tart to nearly a thousand men.

Dawn came at 1100 hours. The *Belfast* sent up a star shell to create more light and, again, the crew could see their quarry.

Frank noticed the *Scharnhorst*'s profile changing as he watched it. At first he was unsure why it looked different this time as it turned away. Then he understood. The German battleship was not turning away. It was moving in to attack.

The enemy ship came for them. All guns blazing.

Again the *Belfast* – as well as the *Sheffield* and *Norfolk* – unleashed their broadsides, hundreds of shells fired across miles of sea at the *Scharnhorst*. Frank counted nine 12-gun assaults from their ship alone.

The noise was monstrous. His head pounded.

The sky seemed to be on fire. But not with the wonder of the aurora borealis. Huge shells rained

down on the three Royal Navy cruisers. Shells the size of a man, filled with enough explosives to sink one ship with one strike in one second.

Frank understood any moment could be his last. And he wouldn't even see his death coming. He might hear it a half-second before the end. But that would be all.

Instead of cowering and giving in to fear, Frank watched in awe as the *Scharnhorst* pulsed, sending arcs of fire across the sea. Watched as the three British cruisers moved towards – not away – from it. The Royal Navy was not backing down.

He scanned the sea for U-boats. He watched for everything. For shells, for mines, for drowning men.

But nothing could have readied him for the shell that fell, screaming like an asteroid from another planet, striking HMS *Norfolk*, a ball of fire skimming across the sea as the *Belfast*'s sister ship

rocked and burned in the darkness. The *Norfolk* was hit, sailors hurling themselves into the water. And the *Sheffield* was way behind. So far back, Frank had lost sight of it. It was either hit or suffering some form of engine failure.

The battle was going badly for the Royal Navy. Very badly. But now the *Scharnhorst* was coming under heavy fire from the *Belfast* and Frank watched as the German warship turned to flee south.

There was time to take a breath, to calm his mind and hammering heart. HMS *Belfast* would surely wait now. Wait to see if its sister ships could continue the fight. The captain wouldn't go it alone against such a formidable enemy, would he?

But to his surprise Frank then felt the propellers churning hard and sensed the change in direction as the *Belfast* accelerated.

"We're going after them," a voice called.

Frank knew that whoever had spoken was right. HMS *Belfast* had left its sister ships behind and was steaming hard to the south in pursuit of the *Scharnhorst*.

The German battleship was running away.

Really?

But why? The Germans knew they had finished the *Norfolk* and that the *Sheffield* had disappeared from the chase. Finish the *Belfast* – the last enemy ship in the area – and it could sink the entire convoy one by one, sending planes and tanks and fuel to the bottom of the sea.

As the *Belfast* pursued the *Scharnhorst* alone, pounding it with all its guns, Frank held on to his binoculars with genuine fear. But he knew he had a job to do and he would do it.

Watch the *Scharnhorst*. See if it begins to turn again. Warn the bridge that the *Scharnhorst* had

set an appalling trap and was turning to come and finish them off.

He felt like the whole war depended on this moment.

TWENTY-TWO

HMS *Belfast* ploughed through the Arctic seas as afternoon became evening, darkness became darker, and cold became frost became ice.

Still on Action Stations, Frank was freezing cold and hungry, though a corned-beef sandwich and an extra tot of rum helped steady his nerves as they continued to pursue the *Scharnhorst*. On its tail. Knowing that the German warship could turn at any point. That it *would* turn. A ship like that didn't just run away. It didn't need to.

And another thing: the captain didn't give out extra tots of rum in the dark because it was

someone's birthday. He did it to give the men courage before battle. That was what rum was for. They all knew it. Just as the soldiers going over the top at the Battle of the Somme had known it.

Then suddenly another star shell exploded. As usual Frank covered his eyes. There was a blinding light above them. Like something out of the Bible. For a second, a half-second, he was dazzled and confused. But then he was back where he should be, doing his job, the waves lit up by a star shell from the *Belfast*.

Frank saw miles of churning sea, the underside of fast scudding clouds racing towards the Russian landmass. He spotted the *Scharnhorst* four miles ahead of them. The German ship had stopped and turned. Ready for their duel.

This was it. The climax.

HMS *Belfast* faced the *Scharnhorst*. It would be a fight to the death. One on one.

But now – cast in the light of the star shell – Frank saw that it was no longer one on one: he spotted two more ships on the far side of the *Scharnhorst*.

So, it *was* a trap. The Germans had lured HMS *Belfast* into a battle with impossible odds. Frank felt a rush of adrenaline.

Fear.

For a moment.

Then it passed and was replaced by another feeling.

Euphoria – as Frank identified the two other ships he knew like old friends.

HMS *Jamaica*.

HMS *Duke of York*.

Yes, it was a trap.

But a trap for the Germans.

Frank heard cheering from other parts of the

deck. Men at their own lookout positions or manning guns, seeing what he saw too.

The *Scharnhorst* would have thought it was luring the *Belfast* alone so that it could destroy her. But now the German giant was alone and surrounded by some of the most well-armed ships on the seas.

Frank felt another rush of adrenaline. A heat going through him even though it was minus 23 degrees.

This was it.

But there was no time to think. Events were taking over. All Frank could do was report what he saw. And what he saw next terrified him. To the starboard side a great plume of water suddenly flashed under the lights, water caught on the wind, thrashing the deck of HMS *Belfast*.

They were under fire. The odds might be 3–1, but there was no guarantee of victory.

Frank studied the *Scharnhorst* through his

binoculars. He knew that the German ship would have seen exactly where the shell had landed. It had only been a hundred metres short at most. Their next shot would be closer – a small adjustment by the German gunner to carry one of its massive fourteen-inch shells that little bit further. It was only a matter of time before they were hit. And one hit in the right place could rip the *Belfast* in two.

Now – just in time – HMS *York* and then HMS *Jamaica* unleashed a monstrous barrage of fire upon the enemy. It was like a firework display. Reds, oranges, yellows and bright burning white reflecting off the sea and the sky and back again.

Frank tried to keep his eyes on the seas around them. Could there be U-boats slithering through the dark waves, waiting to fire secret torpedoes into the hull of the *Belfast*? His job was to spot them.

But it was hard not to look at the *Scharnhorst*.

Because it was burning. The whole ship. It was an awesome sight.

A terrible sight.

But Frank grinned as he saw it.

The wave of euphoria hit him like a broadside until Frank noticed that the German battleship was getting larger. This could signify only one thing: the *Belfast* was moving towards the *Scharnhorst* as it burned.

He could also see that the enemy ship was still giving off fire. Shells were whipping over Frank's head, plunging into the sea, sending up great jets of water as the German battleship tried to put HMS *Belfast*, the smallest of its tormentors, out of action.

Frank was horrified. What was going on? If they got any closer, the *Scharnhorst* could hit them. They were not safe – there was nothing more dangerous or reckless than an injured beast.

Faster and faster they headed towards the wounded battleship. And then a great vibration shuddered up the length of HMS *Belfast*. Frank watched in awe and took in the cheering around him as two threads appeared just under the surface of the water shooting away, two torpedoes heading towards the *Scharnhorst*.

And as he followed the tracks of the two torpedoes, Frank thought of Joseph. He wished his friend could be at his side now seeing what he was seeing. A moment of victory for the Allies. For Russia as well as Britain. He'd be happy about that, wouldn't he?

Now the *Belfast* turned sharply to avoid colliding with the enemy, but not before the crew could watch the *Scharnhorst* take one of the torpedoes full on.

Frank, at his post, saw it all. Reported the hit.

Flashes of orange, great sprays of water, the *Scharnhorst* jerking upwards, then four seconds later a boom. And the great floating city that had filled Frank with fear was on its end, its hull high in the water, slowly sliding down, accompanied by the cheers and whoops of the victorious crew of HMS *Belfast* who knew that they were safe now, that they would live, that they had won.

The cheering went on as HMS *Belfast* turned in a slow arc to avoid running too close to the stricken *Scharnhorst*. Side-on to the German battleship, Frank and the rest of the crew could see what was left of her.

Nothing.

Frank stopped cheering. As did his shipmates. Now there was silence, except for the moaning of the wind.

The *Scharnhorst* was gone. Just gone. Swallowed

up by the black sea beneath the black sky and its blazing stars.

On the surface of the water, the crew of HMS *Belfast* could see another constellation. Hundreds of tiny pinpricks of red light undulating as the waves lifted and dropped them.

Each red light was a man who had managed to escape from inside the *Scharnhorst* before it plunged down to the bottom of the ocean. Men who were now floating on the surface of the freezing ocean.

Frank peered out. He knew that many of the German sailors would be dead already.

Frozen by sub-zero temperatures.

Suffocated by the oil.

Drowned by the waves. And those still alive did not have much time. A lucky few might live long enough to be picked up by the Royal Navy.

Most wouldn't.

AUTHOR'S NOTE

Only thirty-six of the two thousand German sailors on the *Scharnhorst* could be rescued by the Royal Navy.

The dogged confrontation in which Frank and Stephen served and which ended in the sinking of the *Scharnhorst* became known as the Battle of North Cape. As part of my research for writing this story I listened to dozens of hours of recordings of the men who took part in the battle as well as reading everything I could find about it and visiting HMS *Belfast* and the Arctic Convoy Museum in Scotland to be able to tell their story.

One of the most powerful memories recounted by the men on the Royal Navy ships who witnessed the sinking of the *Scharnhorst* is of how their emotions of relief at winning the battle and surviving it faded very quickly as they realised almost instantly how very few of the sailors on board the *Scharnhorst* would survive.

There was a long-established respect between the navies of Britain and Germany, which endured even though

they were now enemies pitted against each other. There was also a sense of empathy. This was best captured by one of the sailors from HMS *Belfast* who took part in the battle, Ted Cordery, who recalled his feeling of regret for the lives lost, just like Frank experienced:

> *We spent two days shadowing* Scharnhorst *and eventually she was sunk. I fired three torpedoes at* Scharnhorst. *It was so dark, whether they hit or not she went down not too long afterwards. And when she went down I had tears in my eyes, because she had two thousand men with her. All with mothers, brothers, sisters, wives, and I thought – what a waste. But, faced with circumstances, it could have been us and not them.*

After the battle, it became clear that as well as the ships mentioned here, there were others involved in the confrontation. But I have written the story from the point of view of those on HMS *Belfast* and what they saw and believed at the time. For instance, it is likely that torpedoes from another ship dealt the fatal blow to the *Scharnhorst.*

The death of almost two thousand aboard the *Scharnhorst* was a tragedy. But it did help bring the Second World War closer to an end, saving millions from having to endure more war, death, slavery and suffering.

HMS *Belfast* went on to take part in another hugely significant battle when, on 6 June 1944, it helped with the D-Day invasions, giving Allied armies a foothold in occupied Europe, leading to the liberation of France and other countries.

It took a long campaign for the men who served on the Arctic Convoys to receive recognition for the particularly harsh conditions they had to endure on what Churchill described as "the worst journey in the world". Veterans initially received the Atlantic Star and it was not until 2013, many decades after the war had ended, that they received an honour intended to reflect the unique circumstances of their service.

The Prime Minister at the time said to the men in a speech at the medal ceremony:

> *You were involved in the most important struggle of the last hundred years, when you were supplying one of our allies in the battle to defeat Hitler and to defeat Fascism in Europe.*

And you showed incredible bravery; incredible courage; against incredible odds.

For someone of my age and of my generation who've seen none of that sort of struggle, we feel completely unworthy and inadequate in the presence of people who risked so much to make sure that we could live in freedom. So, from the bottom of my heart, a really big thank-you, not just from me but from everyone in our country for what you did in those incredibly difficult days, incredibly difficult years, against such appalling odds. You're real heroes.

The medal – pictured opposite – was called the Arctic Star.

Seamen on the quarterdeck of HMS *Belfast*, November 1943.

Onboard the ice-encrusted HMS *Belfast*, November 1943.

HMS BELFAST

HMS *Belfast* was built in the city from which she got her name, Belfast, and launched in March 1938. She was nearly 200 metres long and weighed 11,550 tons.

In August 1939 she was commissioned, which means that she completed all her trials and was accepted for active service in the Royal Navy. This was less than a month before the Second World War began, so her crew moved quickly from performing sea trials to hunting down German enemy ships.

In November of the same year HMS *Belfast* hit a magnetic mine in the Firth of Forth and suffered serious damage. Twenty men ended up in hospital as a result of the explosion, one of whom later died, and twenty-six others suffered minor injuries. The ship was taken to Devonport Docks in Plymouth for repairs.

HMS *Belfast* went on to protect Allied shipping taking supplies to the Russian ports of Murmansk and Archangelsk. Those journeys became known as the

Arctic Convoys. She played a major role in the Battle of North Cape in December 1943, helping to defeat the German warship, *Scharnhorst*.

On D-Day, 6 June 1944, HMS *Belfast* helped lead the opening bombardment of the Allied invasion of Nazi-occupied France as part of Operation Overlord.

In June 1950 the Korean War broke out when North Korean forces invaded South Korea. HMS *Belfast* blockaded the North Korean coast and shelled targets on shore to help the South Korean and United Nations forces who were fighting on land.

The Korean War was the ship's last active period of service before being decommissioned in August 1963. In 1978 she was opened as a museum and is now one of the main sites of the UK's Imperial War Museums.

You can visit HMS *Belfast* where she is docked on the River Thames across from the Tower of London. There you can explore the ship's bridges, the mess decks, the galley and even sleep over as part of an on-board *Kip in a ship*.

For more information, visit
www.iwm.org.uk/visits/hms-belfast/about

Signal lights being used on an Arctic Convoy.

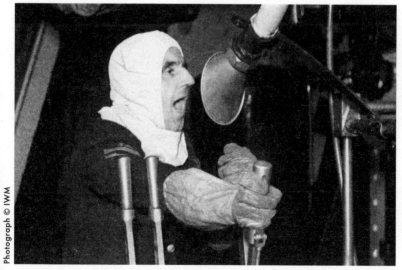

The captain of the gun on HMS *Duke of York*, speaking through the tubes after the sinking of the *Scharnhorst*.

THANKS

Lots of people have helped me write this book. This is my opportunity to thank them.

First and foremost is my editor, Ailsa Bathgate. Since Ailsa arrived at Barrington Stoke, I have never felt so challenged and never worked so hard on my books. I have never felt so proud of them either. That is down to Ailsa. Thank you so much. You are the Marcelo Bielsa of children's literature.

My wife – Rebecca – helps with every book I write. Talking through ideas and making excellent suggestions along the way. Rebecca used to work on HMS *Belfast* and it was her idea that I should look into its history to find a story.

Thank you also to Ngaire Bushell and the rest of the staff at Imperial War Museums. Ngaire helped me with ideas and sources and even gave me a private tour of HMS *Belfast*, telling me lots of fantastic stories as we went round the ship's decks. Ngaire also read the manuscript for me to help me get my facts right to honour those involved in the Arctic Convoys.

This book is dedicated to Imperial War Museums and its staff. I have used the free resources of the museums and benefited from employees' good will and passion for their subject in several books now and I am quite sure I could not have written

Over the Line, *Armistice Runner*, *D-Day Dog*, *After the War* and *Arctic Star* half as well without them being there.

To Julia Hale and Graham Naylor at Plymouth Libraries, who gave me advice on Plymouth now and then, sending me resources that I could use and tips on the city at a time when – during lockdown – I was unable to revisit.

Thank you to the Arctic Convoy Museum and its staff, especially Francis Russell, who kindly read the manuscript and gave me some excellent technical feedback. You can visit the museum on Loch Ewe in the north-west corner of Scotland to find out more about the Arctic Convoys. Their website is also a great source of information: www.racmp.co.uk.

Thank you also to interested friends who read and gave feedback on the manuscript: Rob Power, Jim Sells and his father, David, who served in the Merchant Navy, and Mark Stevo.

Huge thanks to Simon Robinson who read the book three times at different stages and gave me honest feedback. You do so much to help me make my books better than they would have been.

Finally, I would like to thank and pay my respects to the men who sailed on the Arctic Convoys. As I researched what you went through I was in awe of what you endured. I hope this books goes some way to redressing the balance of stories about the Navy when it comes to books about the Armed Forces.